TUDOR STAR

Meg Dawlish becomes companion to Lady Penelope Rich whom she loves and admires. Her mistress, unhappily married, meets the two loves of her life — Sir Philip Sidney, and Sir Charles Blount . . . Meg partakes in the excitement of the Accession Day Tilts and visits the house of the Earl of Essex . . . When Meg falls in love she has to decide whether to leave her mistress and life at court, and follow her lover to the wilds of Shropshire.

SARA JUDGE

TUDOR STAR

Complete and Unabridged

LINFORD
Leicester

First published in Great Britain in 1989 by
Robert Hale Limited
London

First Linford Edition
published 2006
by arrangement with
Robert Hale Limited
London

British Library CIP Data

Judge, Sara
    Tudor star.—Large print ed.—
Linford romance library
    1. Love stories
    2. Large type books
    I. Title
    823.9′14 [F]

ISBN 1–84617–219–5

Published by
F. A. Thorpe (Publishing)
Anstey, Leicestershire
Set by Words & Graphics Ltd.
Anstey, Leicestershire
Printed and bound in Great Britain by
T. J. International Ltd., Padstow, Cornwall

This book is printed on acid-free paper

To my good friend, Ro

To my love Tree ???

1

I began my attendance on Lady Penelope Rich in the January of 1582. She was a lovely lady, possessing beautiful golden hair and black eyes, a most unusual combination. No wonder so many men adored her, and women, too, for Lady Penelope had the kindest heart and was most generous and loving to everyone; her servants, her friends, and her family.

Perhaps it was her husband, Lord Rich, who gained least from her warmth. But then he was liked by few, if any, people, and used my lady for what she could gain for him at Court.

But I digress. First let me go back in time, back to those early years of my childhood, back to the beginning of my life; and pass through all the strange and wonderful things which befell me, Margaret Dawlish, originally from

Cheapside in the City of London.

I did not know my mother for she died, poor lady, whilst bringing me into the world.

But Father I remember quite well, with his thick white hair, and white beard and moustaches beneath very blue, very bright eyes. His eyes dimmed toward the end and became pale and red-rimmed through the pain he had to suffer, but fortunately for him, although not for me, he was not made to suffer long.

Father died in 1576, when I was nine years old, and his death was a great sorrow to me for I had known nothing but happiness up till then.

Kate Haddock was my loving companion, taking care of me from the moment my mother died, and she was a big, well-fleshed woman with rosy cheeks, and eyes as black and sparkling as her mass of hair.

I sometimes wondered if dear Kate had Spanish blood in her veins, so dark was she, but since the death of Queen

Mary, whom some called Bloody, and the coming of our strong Elizabeth to the throne of England, the country of Spain was not admired, nor was Spanish blood to be praised, or desired.

Kate had never married, and when I asked her once why she had not, she laughed and cuddled me close to her, saying that looking after me was all that she wanted in life.

And a good thing for me it was to have Kate Haddock, for she saved my life, I believe, and cared for me as tenderly as any mother could have done.

As I said before, those early years were filled with happiness. I had my father who adored me, his only child, and a daughter, at that. But the fact that I was not a son did not seem to perturb him.

'A beautiful little girl,' he used to say, holding me upon his knee and allowing me to play with the round, golden watch attached to a gold chain, which hung around his neck. 'I have been blessed with a girl-child, as beautiful as her mother — God rest her soul — and with whose company I shall grow old with joy, and contentment, and pride. Why should I want a boy, my darling, when I have you?'

Dear, kind man he was, and so proud of me always. Having me dressed in the finest gowns, and shoes; teaching me, himself, to read and write my letters.

'For my daughter must know about the household and the shop accounts, and must see that bills are paid on time, and that no dishonest wretch can steal one penny from the business through sly miscounting.'

So I learned my figures from him, also, and could write a fair hand and manage most words by the age of seven. Kate was proud of me, Father was proud of me, and I loved them both.

The home we had in Cheapside was above a thriving shop, for Father was a merchant of cloth and brought many lustrous fabrics back from the continent, and the East. He had travelled much in his youth, but now left the sailing to younger men, who were fit and strong and better able to face the hazardous journeys across foreign seas.

For the first seven years my life was perfect, then Father married again and I think it was probably for me that he brought this new, young female into our midst. He was an old man then, well past fifty, and his health was failing although he did not let me see how greatly pain affected him at times. Kate knew, and understood better than I did, for I was young and selfish, yes, and spoilt, and resented this extra female in the household who took up much of Father's time, and was striking in her beauty, which did not endear her to me, either.

Kate did not like this new Mistress Gwendoline, as I found out later, but to begin with she was pleased at the change in our lives, for she realised that my father would not live for many more years, and she had worried about my future as an orphan.

As it turned out, I would have fared better as an orphan, for Mistress Gwendoline married Father for his money, and when she found out that his wealth and possessions had been willed to his only daughter, she was not pleased.

I knew nothing of this at the time for I was too young to understand about wills and inheritance. I knew only that I did not like this young and attractive female, who dressed every day in a new gown, and had her hair frizzed and decorated with precious stones, looking on occasion like the Queen, herself. Mistress Gwendoline possessed yellow eyes, like a cat, and a very white skin, and her hats were often so highly crowned and feathered that she had trouble getting her head-pieces in and out of the various rooms, for the ceilings were low in our Cheapside house.

However, Father appeared pleased

with his choice of bride, and still managed to spend time with me, so life progressed easily enough until he died.

Then everything changed for me and Kate. My dear friend and companion became silent, even irritable with me, and I was not at my best for I missed Father and became cross and unhappy myself.

Mistress Gwendoline, whom I could never make myself call Mother, began entertaining and having friends and young men to the house in unseemly haste once she was widowed, and Kate, who was as intelligent as she was affectionate, listened to conversations which she was not meant to hear.

'We must go away from London,' she told me, as we lay together one night in the big four-poster bed we shared. Her lips were against my tangled hair, and she held me very close to her warm body. 'You must do exactly as I tell you, Margaret, and not question anything. But I fear for your life, my darling, and cannot think of anything else to do, save escape. We must get away from here as soon as possible. Trust me, and you will come to no harm, I promise.'

I was amazed and excited. Life had changed greatly during the past months and I would be glad to start a new life away from Mistress Gwendoline and her roistering friends, so long as Kate remained with me.

Some of the servants had changed; Mistress Gwendoline had brought a new cook into the household, and a different man was now in charge of the shop downstairs. There was no one to hear me reading, or to supervise my writing, for Kate could neither read nor write, and I missed the conversations which I used to have every evening with Father. I was expected to remain in the bedchamber with Kate, and if we went outside we were told to take the kitchen stairs, for Mistress Gwendoline did not want me interrupting her visitors, who always occupied the best rooms upstairs.

'Kate,' I said, putting my arms

around her big body and clinging to her, 'I will go wherever you take me and be thankful. I do not like it here in Cheapside any more.'

Why she should fear for my life I did not bother to ask. It was enough that I trusted Kate, and would do whatever she asked of me.

On a bright sunny afternoon in September of that year 1576, Kate and I arrived at Leighs Priory in Essex, and began our lives on the great estate belonging to Lord Rich.

We lived with Ann and George Tredworthy in rooms above the stables. Ann was Kate's younger sister and was one of the laundry women for the big house. Her husband, George, was a groom.

I enjoyed my years with the Tredworthys, for they were kind people with a growing family, and although we all worked very hard there was happiness and good humour in abundance.

Kate began at once helping her sister with the washing, and I was introduced to the Tredworthys' eldest daughter and told to help her with the younger ones. Mary was very pleased to have me with her in those two rooms above the stables, for her mother seemed able to produce a new baby every year. Despite this, she never stayed at home for long but within a week of the birth she would be off to the laundry rooms again, on the other side of the courtyard, bearing the newest arrival strapped to her back so that she could feed it at odd moments of the day. Mary and I took care of the others, and prepared the main meal of the day which was eaten when Ann and Kate and George returned home after work.

It was very vigorous, very physical work for me, to which I was not accustomed, but I was young and healthy and happy to be with a family who showed affection to each other, and who welcomed me as if I were one of them.

I felt safe there, needed and loved, but my greatest enjoyment was in observing all the to-ing and fro-ing at the big house, wondering what the rooms and furnishings were like inside, and how many people lived in such a huge establishment.

There was a great stone archway beside the stable block to the west, through which the horses arrived to enter the vast courtyard beyond, and right through the centre of the house was another archway, like a passage, which led out to the east side and the gardens beyond.

George Tredworthy told us that Leighs Priory had once been a monastery, hence its name, and the dwelling had been given to the present Lord Rich's grandfather by King Henry VIII. Sir Richard Rich had been Lord Chancellor of England, and he amassed great wealth for his family, mainly by the dissolving of religious houses.

The present Lord Rich was not married, but he was looking for a bride, and this fact also interested and excited me. I soon forgot about Mistress

Gwendoline and my life in Cheapside, and looked forward to joining Kate and Ann in the laundry rooms once I was older.

My one great longing was to get inside that magnificent dwelling-place and see how noble folk lived, and as the laundry women took it in turns to return the cleaned and ironed linen to the big house, I felt sure that once I worked with them I, too, would gain entrance to the inside of Leighs Priory.

I saw Lord Rich on a few occasions, riding in and out of the courtyard, but I did not find him a romantic figure. He was small and cross-faced, and George Tredworthy told me that his master possessed a violent temper, and all the servants went in fear of him.

I felt sorry for the lady who would eventually marry such a man, remembering my father and his gentle voice, and unending patience, but presumably wealth and possessions would make up for Lord Rich's unpleasant character.

One fact which annoyed Kate very

much was that Lord Rich was a Puritan, and expected everyone on his estate to practise the religion which he supported.

'I can accept the Reformed church as it is, for our Queen has taken it to her heart,' I heard her say to Ann Tredworthy soon after we arrived in Essex, 'and life in London certainly seemed better and happier than the way I heard it was under her Catholic sister, Queen Mary. We do not want to be like the Spanish, as my old master used to say. But this Puritan business is really too much with its dislike of card games and play-going, and even dancing and *music* are looked upon as vices. I ask you, Ann, are we to have no joy in our lives?'

Ann shrugged her shoulders and then lifted her newest babe and held it to her breast.

'They say the Queen loves dancing,' she replied, 'and if such amusements are allowed at Court, why should the ordinary folk not take part in such activities also, when they have a moment free from their toils? I must admit that I do not understand the Puritans, but whilst you remain with us it is safer and better to do what is required. Every Sunday we are expected to go to the Hall, Kate, and listen to the preacher.'

Kate snorted. 'I went with you last week and could not believe my ears. Not one word from the Prayer Book, no lovely singing of the psalms, just the minister's voice denouncing everything I most enjoy in life! Well,' she thrust her hands onto her wide hips and glanced sideways at me, 'I will keep going as you suggest, but I'll not let Margaret into such a pious and miserable place. She can stay here and look after the babes and she'll be happier for that, I have no doubt.'

All the talk about Catholics and Puritans meant nothing to me then, but the Hall did not sound a welcoming place so I was glad to remain at home with Mary and the younger children,

when Kate and the Tredworthys went
out every Sunday evening.

★　★　★

I believe that Fate decreed my first
meeting with Lady Penelope Rich for,
despite my earlier hopes, I had never
been able to enter Leighs Priory. When
I was older I did join Kate and Ann in
the laundry rooms, washing and scrub-
bing with them until my poor hands
became scarlet with the heat and wet.
But because I was the newest, and the
youngest girl there, I was not allowed
the honour of returning clean linen to
the house. This was a great privilege
allowed to only the most skilled and
experienced of laundry women, and I
was not one of them.

Kate had been once. She had been
given a bowl of soup in the great
kitchen afterwards, for it was a
particularly perishing winter's day, and
she told me of the high vaulted ceiling
with four central arches which held the

hearths; the huge brick oven for baking, and the magnificent array of pot-racks, posnetts and chafing-dishes; knives, cleaver axes and pot-hooks; kneading troughs, fire-shovels and gridirons all hanging upon the walls.

'The squillerie was next door,' she told me, 'and I had a peek in there before coming away and, Meg, it made me thankful that I did not have to prepare meals for such a great household. There were so many brass pots and pans and pewter vessels there, that with those, and the many articles in the kitchen, the servants must be forever either filling them up, or emptying and cleaning them ready for the next meal!'

The house was so vast, she said, she had followed a man-servant up the stairs and along numerous passages, carrying her basket of clean washing, until they finally reached the big room where the linen was stored in great, carved, Cyprus wood chests.

I was both envious and bitter, longing

for the thing I could not have. Then one day Fate took a hand and my wish was granted.

In November of the year 1581 Lord Rich married Lady Penelope Devereux in London.

Lady Penelope was a maid of honour to the Queen, and she continued with her attendances at Court after her marriage so we saw little of her at Leighs Priory. But occasionally she would ride out to Essex, and it was on one of these brief visits that the miraculous thing happened.

Mary had not been well that week, she was very feverish and flushed, as were two of the younger ones, and so I had not gone to the laundry but had stayed at home to look after the sick children.

Whilst I was attending to Mary and washing her poor, burning forehead with a damp cloth, the oldest and brightest boy, named Jimmy, took it upon himself to vanish.

Suddenly I heard Rosie calling out

— 'He's gone to see the horses!'

Above her voice I heard the thundering of horses' hooves and, running to the back window, I saw a cavalcade of horsemen coming down the track which led to Leighs Priory. Jimmy was nowhere to be seen, but I knew that a small boy would have little chance if he moved in front of such a troop. Leaving Mary and the others alone, I ran out through the door which led to the stairs, and down them at the back of the stables. None of the children were allowed through the archway which led to the vast courtyard, but I had a terrible fear that Jimmy had gone that way.

I let the cavalcade pass by and then followed under the archway to look for Jimmy. Then out from the darkness of an empty stable I saw his little figure emerge and run towards the group who were reining up and dismounting in front of the house. Grooms and stable lads were everywhere, and I prayed that someone would see Jimmy and stop him from getting too close to the horses.

Suddenly, one of the beasts took fright and reared away from the lad holding it. It turned and began cantering wildly towards me, and in my path was Jimmy. I screamed at him to get out of the way, which he must have managed to do, for the horse missed him but knocked me down in its panic-stricken flight.

Rough hands pulled me to my feet and I could hear voices, George Tredworthy's amongst them, but was so winded and shocked I could not say anything myself. Then another voice spoke, a clear, crisp female voice, and the group fell back around me leaving one man's arms supporting me from behind.

'Are you hurt?' I heard the sweet voice ask. 'Gracious me, you might have been killed. Take her up to my chamber at once,' she ordered, as I lolled ungracefully before her, unable to show my gratitude. 'Will, carry her up. At once, I say.'

I was lifted in powerful arms and carried across the courtyard, through endless doorways and passages and up a staircase, until we reached a big room with lavish wall-hangings, and a huge four-poster bed in the middle of it.

'There.' I was laid none too gently upon a truckle-bed near the window, and a bearded face looked down at me. 'My Lady Rich will be with you shortly. How fortunate for you that my lady saw you, and not Lord Rich.'

I had time to stare at my new surroundings once sense returned to my brain, and was immediately impressed by the size of the great bed. This was most beautifully carved all over the top, and the back, which enclosed the head from post to post, was lavishly decorated with intricate designs, as were the two foot-posts. The coverlet was of blue damask, and there were fine tapestries upon the walls depicting strange beasts, woven in blue and red, green and gold.

The smell of the bedchamber was very pleasing, and I could tell that there were many herbs amongst the strewn rushes, particularly lavender and rosemary.

Even as I lay there, forgetting my pain in the amazement at what I saw around me, Lady Penelope Rich entered the room.

2

The very first time I saw Lady Penelope I loved her. She was so beautiful with her fair, golden hair and dark brown eyes. She was bright, sparkling with a joy of living and a laugh upon her lips as if the whole world delighted her. And yet, despite the continual good humour, she was kind and caring so that one felt immediately that she wanted everyone whom she met to be as happy as she was. She was intelligent and able, as I learned later, to talk to the cleverest of men in their own way, and she could speak French and Italian and Spanish fluently.

Of course I could not know all this on that first January day at Leighs Priory, but I could see that she was lovely; I could hear her clear, bright voice and watch those enchanting black eyes, which looked at me with concern and tenderness.

'There now, rest and regain your energy, little one,' she said, when she joined me in the upper chamber. 'Do you think a bone has been broken, or are you only bruised?'

'Only bruised, thank you, my lady,' I whispered, overwhelmed that such an important person should be interested in me.

'Then tell me your name and let us get to know one another.' She handed her cloak and gloves to the maid who had followed her. 'Bring us Gossip's Cup and saffron cakes, Nell,' she said, 'and send word to the master that I will see him this evening.'

The maid curtseyed and went out, leaving us alone together.

Lady Penelope was wearing a gown of russet velvet, with a round neck, low at her bosom and edged with lace. There was lace at her wrists, and the long russet sleeves were trimmed with brown satin ribbons. A small white ruff encircled her long neck, and on her head she wore a tall-crowned hat trimmed with pearls and feathers. There were pearls, also, buttoned on her bodice, and on the belt around her slender waist.

I stared in wonder for I had not seen such finery since leaving Mistress Gwendoline in London many years before.

Once I had told my name and my age and where I lived, for she must know it all, she laughed and placed a hand gently on my shoulder.

'Dear Margaret,' she said, 'do you like fine clothes so much? I can see your eyes devouring my garments as if you would eat them, given the chance. Poor lamb, do you have better clothes for Sundays? Or are all your dresses as thread-bare as the one you are wearing today?'

'They are both like this.'

I glanced down at the stained and darned kirtle on my body and realised that I had worn it for weeks, without thought of changing to the other one I possessed.

'We are so busy with the washing for the big house, my lady, there is little time to worry about what we have on,' I tried to explain.

Not that it mattered with the Tredworthys. So long as we were warm enough, and the holes and torn places were not too large, letting in the winter's draughts, we did not bother about what garments covered our grubby forms. Indeed, a change of clothing was unusual above the stables; with so many children about, every piece of cloth was used and re-used and continually mended.

I stared at my companion's long slim fingers which were encrusted with several jewelled rings, and saw that the skin on her hands, and on her face, was as pure and gleaming fresh as newly fallen snow.

'Kate always kept me nice and clean in London,' I blurted out, suddenly ashamed of my appearance. 'It is only since we came to Essex that we have not been able to live up to the standards we once knew.'

'You came from London originally?' Lady Penelope raised her brows. 'And from a well-bred and educated household at that, if my ears do not deceive me. Tell me, Margaret, have you learned how to read and write?'

I nodded. 'But I have not done anything like that for several years, my lady. It was my father who taught me and he has been dead since 1576.'

My companion's eyes darkened further as she looked at me.

'1576? How strange. That is the very year in which my dear father died.' She turned her head away and gazed out of the window which was set into the wall above where I lay. 'In Ireland, and some say it was due to poison.' Then she lifted her shoulders in a light shrug and glanced back at me. 'No matter, it is all in the past now. So Kate is not your mother, I presume?'

I shook my head. 'Kate is a very good and kind friend, as good as any mother,' I said warmly. 'She has cared for me since my birth because my mother died then.'

'Poor Margaret.' Lady Penelope patted my shoulder again and her eyes softened with sympathy. 'I am fortunate in having a mother whom I love most dearly, but I can understand how hard it must be to have neither parent on whom to lean in times of trouble, or distress. Have you brothers, or sisters, Margaret?'

'None.'

'And I have been blessed with three. Oh, I can see the question on your face but you do not dare to ask! Come, Margaret, if we are to be friends, and somehow I have the strangest feeling that our lives are to be linked from now on — then please, dear Meg — I shall call you that, if I may? Please, let us not have secrets from one another. If there is something you wish to know, I beg of you — *ask!*

'My brothers, Meg, are named Robert and Walter, and my dearest sister, who is next in age to me, is called Dorothy.'

At that moment Nell returned with goblets of silver, and the saffron cakes, and very good it all was, too. I was not used to eating in the middle of the day, for we ate some bread before leaving for the laundry rooms every morning, and Mary had our main meal ready for us when we returned of an evening. But now, talking to this wonderful lady, and lying warm and comfortable upon the truckle-bed within the very heart of Leighs Priory, I was able to eat and drink with relish.

Later, I was to grow accustomed to many fine wines and meats, but the memory of that first sip of Gossip's Cup, in the company of Lady Penelope Rich, never faded from my mind. In fact, I was to learn from my lady how this excellent drink was made and, it being such a great favourite of mine, the Gossip's Cup which I first tasted aged fifteen years at Leighs, became the drink produced most often in my own home, many years later.

I remember her voice to this day, that

clear voice, so young then and so excited and pleased about everything in her vivid life.

'I shall tell you how to make it, Meg, and that will be your lesson for today,' she had said, on one of our brief visits to Essex. 'Take cinnamon, white ginger, cloves, nutmeg, grains of Paradise and pepper, and steep them for six days in spirits of wine. A few drops of this added to a bowl of wine makes ypocras — and when you desire your Gossip's Cup, you mix half a pint of ypocras with a bottle of ale.'

Before I left the chamber that January day, it was decided by my benefactress that I should serve her.

'If you are willing, that is?' The black eyes glistened with delight. 'I shall send for your Kate tomorrow, dear Meg, and will have words with her. I have a need for someone young and intelligent to be my travelling-companion, and to help with my dressing. Heaven knows, that takes long enough each day, and several times each day when I am at Court.

Nell is a good kind soul, but happiest here in the country, and I rather feel that you would enjoy some adventure in your young life. Am I right?

'Would you like to accompany me to London? And see the Queen? And learn of all the thrills and intrigues at Court? Ah, I can see that you are dumb-founded!'

She knelt beside the truckle-bed and placed her arms around me, pressing her face against my tangled, dirty hair so that her ruff tickled my cheek.

'Dearest Meg, come with me and we will enjoy ourselves together. If you promise to be good and loyal to me, I shall endeavour to see that you never want for anything, and that the security of your future is assured. *And* you will receive many new and pretty garments,' she added, lifting her head and smiling at me with devilment in her black eyes.

I was sad to leave my faithful Kate, and the Tredworthy family, who had been so kind to me during the past years, but the thought of living a new life, rich with different people, lavish jewels and clothing, and all the splendour and excitement of the Court, did more than ease my mind. It filled my head with ideas which I had never experienced before.

Lady Penelope told both me and Kate that our partings would never be for long, as she would be frequently returning to Leighs Priory, and this knowledge also helped to numb the sorrow of my departure.

We travelled on horseback then, as we were to do most times in the future. Lord Rich owned a great coach, emblazoned with the Rich family arms, but my lady hated it and found it most tiring, with all the jolting and jarring to her body, and the terrible rumbling and squeaking of the wheels.

Once we arrived in London all thoughts of my past life in Essex vanished, for there was so much to see and hear, my days and nights brimmed with new sights and knowledge.

Seeing the Queen for the first time

was a terrifying experience. I only saw her at a distance, for I was of no importance and had to keep well away from the Presence Chamber and the State Apartments, where she and the courtiers met, and danced, and played cards together.

But I saw her outside the Palace of Whitehall at one of the jousting events held during my first week there and later, one evening at a masque, held within the Palace, where many of us servants managed to find a space amongst the crowds.

Queen Elizabeth must have been nearly fifty then, but she was so clever with her face powders and colours that, at the distance from which I observed her, she still looked like a young woman. She was also slim, holding herself very erect in a magnificent gown of gold velvet embroidered with hundreds of lustrous pearls, which helped the girlish image.

Her hair was a strong red, with no hint of grey in it, but Lady Penelope told me later that the Queen possessed a fine assortment of wigs. To my country girl's eyes she looked every inch a queen — bejewelled, magnificently attired, haughtily supreme. And yet, what was it that frightened me about her? Although I saw her many times over the years, I never lost the frightened feeling, that lurch in my heart whenever I was in her presence.

Thinking back now after all that has passed, having experienced both good and bad times with Her Majesty in high good humour, and fiery rages, I believe my fear of her was caused by her apparent lack of human kindness; her sharp black eyes, hooky nose and thin lips made her seem clever, but crafty.

When I first saw my Lady Penelope and looked into her face, I knew that she cared about people, that she was kind. But I could never believe the Queen to be capable of gentle compassion, or tenderness. She loved the Earl of Leicester, of course, and Essex, my lady's handsome young brother, some of the time, and no doubt there were others of whom she was fond. But she never gave an outward impression of caring for others, whereas everyone around her was continually fawning over her.

Lady Penelope said that the Queen's lack of showing affection was due to her difficult early years, with her mother losing her head when Elizabeth was but a babe, and her father not loving her, or even wanting her, because she was not a boy.

This was probably so, but although we all respected her and knew that she was a very fine Queen, we heard continual stories of how vicious she was at times to her attendants, and such knowledge aroused no love in our hearts for our sovereign.

When Her Majesty left Court each summer to go off on one of her annual Progresses through the countryside, it was related that the country folk adored her. We heard that the Queen would stop at villages and hamlets and allow the people to go up to her and tell her of their troubles, or injustices. And in London, also, when Queen Elizabeth rode out, accompanied by her handsome young courtiers all clad in their finest silks and satins, then, too, the townsfolk cheered and waved to her, glorying in such a pageant of riches.

She was a great Prince, no doubt of that, but for those of us who dwelt nearer, and heard continual gossip from her ladies and attendants, she was not a lovable human being.

During my first week at the Palace of Whitehall I learned so much, and was surprised — even astounded — by so many new things, that I almost felt that my brain would burst with such extraordinary happenings.

Apart from the Queen, the other person of great stature was the Earl of Leicester. And after hearing about him, for there was continual chatter and gossip amongst us servants, and learning that he was the Queen's favourite and the most important man at Court,

I was then introduced to him by my Lady Penelope.

Sometimes I did not see my lady for a whole day, for once I had helped her to dress and arranged her hair for her, always at a very early hour, she would scurry off to the Queen's apartments and wait there, with other attendants and maids of honour, until sent for. Sometimes the Queen slept late and at other times she awoke early, but whenever she woke and called for her ladies, they had to be ready and waiting for her command.

I, in turn, must always be ready for Lady Penelope, and as I never knew when she would come hurrying to the little chamber we shared, wanting to be helped out of one gown and into another, I never dared to venture far away from the room. Once she was suitably attired for an outside joust or tournament, or for a banquet inside the Palace, I was able to follow her at a distance, knowing that for a few hours my attentions would not be needed.

Fortunately for my lady, and therefore for me, she possessed the skin and colouring most desired at Court.

'You see, Meg,' she informed me when first I began assisting her, 'I am blessed with a fair complexion and golden hair. You would be astonished at the lengths some ladies go to in order to produce the pink, white, and golden looks so beloved by gentlemen.'

I possessed a white skin, for which I was suddenly most thankful, but my dark brown hair was not a beautiful sight, nor were my eyes which were of a pale brown, touched with yellow. However, not being a lady of importance, and knowing no gentleman whom I wished to impress, my looks did not bother me.

'What can a lady do to improve her colouring?' I asked, padding out Lady Penelope's hair above her temples with silk, and fixing it with silver wire, which was held in place by a cap of lace. This cap cleverly concealed the wire as it was heavily encrusted with pearls.

'They have to paint their skins with white fucus, made from the burned jawbones of a hog or sow, then ground or sieved and laid on the face with white of egg.'

'How dreadful!' I shivered with distaste.

'But remarkably effective,' said my lady. 'Then a rouge and lipsalve produces the required pink and that, so I have been told, is made by mixing cochineal, white of hard-boiled egg, milk of green figs, alum and gum arabic.'

'Goodness me, madam,' I replied, 'how thankful I am that you do not need such requirements for your daily attire.'

Lady Penelope pressed out her glowing pink lips and studied them for a moment in the little silver-backed mirror which hung from a ribbon at her waist.

'I am most fortunate, Meg, in having naturally rosy lips. Such additions to my face would only be needed if I were to fall low with the smallpox. I pray every night that such a dreadful disease will never come my way,' answered my lady soberly.

The day I met the Earl of Leicester, she swept me along with her towards the apartments which I knew to be occupied by the Queen.

'Come, Meg,' my lady said to me, soon after we had arrived at the Palace of Whitehall, 'I want you to meet my stepfather. He is a very active man and always busy with Court matters, so he sees little of my poor mother. But he has agreed that I may take you to him this morning, Meg, so come quickly before he vanishes.'

Within a few minutes I was ushered into the presence of a rather fat man, whose blue eyes gazed directly at me from a broad, somewhat paunchy face. He possessed a dark beard, heavily streaked with grey, and although he was ageing, I could sense that this was a man of enormous prestige.

'So, this is Margaret who will take

care of my Penelope? Guard her well, Meg, and make sure that she is never late for attendance on the Queen.'

I nodded and curtseyed, struck dumb by the piercing eyes and the command of his deep voice. Although the Earl of Leicester was a young man no longer, I was female enough to realise how attractive he must have been formerly, and to know why he had been supreme favourite for so many years. But Lady Penelope's stepfather? I could not understand that. Married to my lady's mother? Then where was she, and how did she feel about her husband's continual presence at Court?

The Earl of Leicester placed an arm around my lady's shoulders and gave her a quick hug.

'Be careful, my dear,' he said gently, looking down at her bright, upturned face. 'For better or worse you are married now and Philip is not for you. I have suffered much from ill-managed affairs of the heart, and would not see you so punished.'

I saw the blood rush to my lady's face as she turned her head away and smiled across at me, somewhat forcedly.

'The Earl and Countess of Leicester have a beautiful baby boy, Meg, so I am possessed of yet another brother. Lord Denbigh, I believe?' She tilted her head to look at Leicester once more. 'You must be a proud father, sir.'

'I am indeed, but we were talking of you, Penelope, and of Philip. I have made it clear that I desire his marriage to your sister, thus uniting our two families yet again, but such a marriage is only desired if love and liking are between them.'

'A pity that such a desire was not expressed during my wedding arrangements, then, my lord,' answered my mistress tartly, and broke away from his embrace. 'Come, Meg, we must not keep this great man from his work. No doubt the Queen will be calling for me soon, and I must be ready and waiting should she require my presence.'

'Goodbye, Penelope, and take care, I

beg you. Meg, see that she behaves herself with the modest behaviour required of Lady Rich.'

I inclined my head and curtseyed further, before following Lady Penelope from the chamber. Much had happened in so short a time that I was totally bemused. Who was this Philip? Why should my lady be warned about him? And where was this sister who was supposed to marry him?

My mind churned with the unanswered questions, but my lady was not in the mood for confidences and no more was learned by me that day. But forget I could not and, remembering Lady Penelope's plea to me back in Essex, to have no secrets from each other, I was determined to ask her all that I longed to know the moment we had the necessary time together.

In truth, I was to learn the identity of the Earl of Leicester's 'Philip' before I had the chance to talk to my lady about him.

3

During one bright day that first spring, I saw the young man whom the Queen had just knighted and, on hearing his name from one of my companions — a girl who, like me, attended one of the maids of honour — I knew at once that this must be Lady Penelope's 'Philip'.

He was now Sir Philip Sidney, and a most handsome and proud courtier he looked, to my admiring eyes. I stared for a long time, taking in every detail of his appearance and knowing immediately the reason for my lady's feelings towards him.

How different was he — courtly, gracious, dark-eyed and dark-haired, with no beard upon his pale face — from the small, unattractive and over-pious Lord Rich.

'Sir Philip has been an ambassador abroad,' explained my friend, Annie, in answer to my many questions. She had been almost two years at Court and knew everything. 'He has travelled widely and is a strong Protestant, which pleases the Queen. He also writes most beautifully, he is a most competent rider at the tilting tournaments, and he is nephew to the Earl of Leicester, on his mother's side.'

I nodded and listened to every word. An admirable young man, tall and slender, as well as being handsome in his doublet of green satin, decorated with tiny slashes of silver. His trunk hose of saffron yellow were well padded above long, slim legs encased in silk stockings and adorned with silver thread. His ruff was narrow, on a stand collar, and on his dark head Sir Philip wore a yellow velvet hat, trimmed with small feathers and several brooches of emerald stones, which matched the green of his doublet.

'At the November tilts he surprised us all by the device upon his shield,' Annie went on. 'His motto had always been 'I hope' but on that day he appeared with the words 'I have hoped' crossed through.'

'Why?' I asked. Was this perhaps showing his love for Lady Penelope thwarted by her marriage to Lord Rich?

My companion shrugged. 'We were not sure, but believe it to have been because he was disinherited. He should have been the Earl of Leicester's heir, but last summer his uncle and new wife produced a son, so that was that for Sir Philip.'

Had Lady Penelope comforted him, I wondered? But if so, it was not a desirable action for a young girl about to be wed to another, and even worse now that she was married to Lord Rich. No wonder the Earl had warned her about her behaviour. She was the Lady Rich now, like it or not, and she should be there, in Essex, playing her part as mistress of the great house.

Yet, remembering Leighs Priory as I did, and comparing it to the Palace of Whitehall, I could not entirely condemn my lady. Here at Court there was so much life and laughter, beauty and pageantry, it was not surprising that a young and vivacious girl should want to stay here in the midst of gaiety and splendour, instead of being buried in the puritanical existence of that Essex household.

'The Earl of Leicester's wife?' I queried, taking my thoughts back to the present and realising that Annie would go on talking indefinitely, if given the chance. 'Is she my Lady Penelope's mother? And why is she never seen at Court?'

'Because she defied the Queen and married the favourite. *Nobody* may marry without Royal Consent, but Lettice Devereux did.'

'But the Earl is allowed here, and remains favourite,' I said, 'that does not seem fair to me. Why was he not blamed as much as his wife?'

'Who knows, Meg, what goes on in the Royal Mind,' answered Annie softly, 'but the Queen loves Leicester, of that there is no doubt, and I do not think she could live without him.'

'And the Countess — how does she feel about this?' It seemed very strange to me, but then Lady Penelope was more often away from her husband than with him. Perhaps this frequent parting from man and wife was quite common in Court circles. And my lady had appeared fond of the Earl of Leicester, and had taken me to be introduced to him. She would surely not have done that if she had felt that he was hurting her mother.

'I believe the Countess of Leicester would dearly like to return to Court,' said Annie, 'for she is a cousin of the Queen's, you know. Doubtless she thinks she has the right to be here. In the old days they were most friendly, so I have been told, and Lettice was one of the Queen's first maids of honour, before she married Devereux. But Her Majesty has banished her now, for marrying the wrong man, and I do not think she will ever be allowed to return to Court.'

How sad, I thought, and how careful one must be to tread through this labyrinth of power, cautious never to offend the Royal Personage.

'Sir Philip Sidney,' I said thoughtfully, 'has he a wife?'

Annie laughed. 'You must know by now that he and your Lady Penelope are in love. Do not put on such innocent airs for me, Meg Dawlish. No, Sir Philip is not married, and we all wait and watch and ponder on the outcome, for your lady never wanted to marry Lord Rich. She protested at the very ceremony itself, and insisted that such a marriage was against her will. But she was only eighteen then, and all her relatives insisted on it so she could do nothing but obey.'

'And the Queen was told, and consented to the marriage?'

'Oh yes, Her Majesty was very much in favour.'

'Poor Lady Penelope, I do hope that she will be careful now. This seems to

be a dangerous place for intrigue. Does
— does Lord Rich ever come to
Court?'

How dreadful if he should find out;
how appalling if he should divorce her!
Oh, the scandal and the shame of it!
And what would she do then? For the
Queen would never keep her at Court.
She expected all her ladies to have
impeccable morals. Maybe her mother
would give her a home? Or would she
be able to marry Sir Philip once the
furore had died down?

'I have never seen Lord Rich here,'
said Annie. 'He is too much of a
Puritan, if you ask me. All the dancing
and singing and card-playing would be
greatly frowned upon. But the Queen is
a different matter, for she has spies
everywhere, and although the girls I
know would be loyal and hold their
tongues, there are countless watching
eyes, Meg, and many tongues would
wag for the reward of a few pence.
Watch your mistress, and be ever on
your guard for her.'

Similar words to the ones I had heard from the great Leicester. Very well. I had been warned, but alas, I was servant to a most headstrong and determined young mistress.

That spring and early summer of 1582, Sir Philip Sidney and my lady saw each other as often as they could, and I was their watch-dog, keeping a lookout for anyone who might intrude upon their stolen moments of happiness. Of course I could not tell Lady Penelope Rich what to do, or how to behave, but I could watch over her, and guard her, in possibly a different way to the one meant by the Earl of Leicester.

Their meetings were infrequent and often short, for both of them could be called for by the Queen at any moment of the day or night, and my duty was to look after my lady as best I could. I made it my business to get to know all the pages, by sight if not by name, and I could recognise them all from a distance and know at once if they were searching for one of my charges.

A favourite trysting-place was out in the gardens, hidden from the Palace by a thick hedge of yew, and another was in the kitchen wing, where storerooms abounded. My lady trusted me to keep watch and to hold my tongue, and both were achieved without difficulty.

The strange thing was that I enjoyed these stolen moments on my own account, for I met a gentleman on one of these vigils, who appeared to enjoy my company, and who seemed always to know where I would be waiting on a certain day, at a certain time.

At first I was scared in case he was a spy, and was unduly curt and unfriendly towards him. But after mentioning his name to my lady, and after she had spoken to Sir Philip about him, I was assured of my gentleman's integrity and allowed myself to talk naturally with him whilst waiting for my lady and Sir Philip to reappear.

His name was Richard Villier, and although he had a home in Shropshire he seemed to spend a great deal of his time at Court. He was a good friend of Sir Philip Sidney and had been with him at Shrewsbury School, then at Oxford.

I found this gentleman both charming and interesting, and once I had let down my guard, talk flowed between us like a fast-running stream. It was Richard Villier who talked, of course, for there was little knowledge in my empty brain, being so young and newly come from the country. But my father's training so long ago had sown curiosity, and a love of learning, in my mind and when I met someone whom I trusted, who was far cleverer than I, and who, moreover, had the time to spend with me, I allowed the questions to pour forth, and he seemed both amused and intrigued by my company.

'Why do you spend so much time with me?' I asked, flattered by his attention but wondering why such an accomplished man should waste precious minutes, sometimes hours, hanging about with a serving-maid.

'Several reasons,' answered Richard, leaning his tall frame back against the wall of the passage where we waited in the kitchen wing, and smiling down at me in the semi-darkness. 'Because your mind is unformed and barren, crying out for food on which to grow and thrive; because, despite your youth, you are avid for knowledge and further education; because you are delightfully innocent and like a breath of fresh air in this steamy atmosphere of scandal and intrigue; and because I find you a very pretty maid and like to look at you.'

This last sentence made me blush in an agony of confusion, for I had never been told that I was seemly before, having taken both Father's loving comments and Kate's endearments as the words of family, who naturally loved me. And I did not possess golden hair.

Yet here was a stranger, and a male at that, who had probably seen hundreds of lovely females during his time at Court and on his travels, who said quite clearly that he found me pretty.

'Do not stand there looking like some rain-sodden blossom drooping from the weight. Look at me and smile that enchanting smile, and ask some more questions if they will ease your mind.'

I swallowed and tilted up my chin, before managing a somewhat creaking —

'For how long were you abroad with Sir Philip?'

'We were away from England for three years and we visited France, and the Emperor Rudolph in Prague. Philip was very proud of the fact that he was an ambassador for the Queen, and we both enjoyed gaining knowledge of other languages, religions, and laws.'

'You are very wise,' I said.

Not only that, but also handsome. If Richard Villier found me attractive then the feeling was mutual. He was taller than Sir Philip, with broader shoulders and a stronger face, but like his friend he wore no beard or whiskers upon his countenance. Richard's hair was also a lighter brown in colour, and he wore it longer, so that it touched the ruff at the back of his neck. His eyes were a clear, light green; unusual eyes, darkly fringed, which appeared to be amused all the time as if life was one long comedy.

'I am not as clever as Philip,' answered my companion slowly. 'If I am not mistaken he is going to be a very great man. Foreigners think the world of him, and people here are now beginning to realise his worth. He is remarkably talented and possesses an excellent mind, full of wit and intelligence.'

'Has he no faults?' I queried, disliking the thought that any young man could be quite so perfect.

'Perhaps he takes himself a little too seriously, that is why he likes to have me by his side as often as possible. I may mock him at times which does him good.'

'And my lady,' I said quickly, 'she has such a sense of fun I cannot believe that anyone could be in her company for long and remain serious.'

Except for Lord Rich, I thought. I had never seen his cross face light up with amusement. But then Lady Penelope was not often in his presence. She was more frequently lighting up Sir Philip Sidney's life.

'Yes, Lady Penelope,' answered Richard Villier, somewhat coldly for him, and I looked at him in surprise.

'Do you not like her?'

'Do not get on your high horse with me, Meg, for I admire your Penelope Rich and like her vivacious manner, which is good for Philip. But I wonder a little what the outcome of this liaison can be, and hope that neither of these two people will be hurt by their present behaviour.'

As Fate would have it, the love-affair between my lady and her knight in shining armour ended abruptly that summer.

Sir Philip Sidney left Court and went to stay with his father in Hereford, far away near the border with Wales, and soon after his departure we returned to Essex to await the arrival of the Richs' first child.

Lady Penelope's first daughter was born in November and she was named Lettice, after her maternal grandmother.

Lord Rich was not very interested in the baby; it was a girl and he, like so many men, desired a son. Lady Penelope would have to do better next time.

But she and I loved little Lettice, and I believe that her birth helped my lady to get over the fact that she would not see Sir Philip Sidney again. At least, not as a lover.

He was busy with his own affairs, and was often at the family home of Penshurst, in Kent. But that summer of 1582 after they had parted, he must have spent a great deal of time in writing. For letters came for my lady that autumn, many of them, and she told me with a glow in her dark eyes, that Sir Philip had written a series of poems for her.

'There are one hundred and eight sonnets, Meg, and eleven songs, and they read like a diary of verse telling the story of our love.'

I marvelled at the time spent on such writing, and although I did not see the written words, my lady often quoted from the poems, or read me parts which particularly impressed her.

'He has titled them 'Astrophil and Stella' and I am Stella, meaning star. Is that not lovely, Meg? And he is lover of the star.'

She held little Lettice to her breast as she spoke, then lowered her head and pressed the babe's downy hair lightly with her lips.

'One of the best lines is in praise of his mistress who — 'hath no misfortune but that Rich she is'. Ah me, how right that is! I am indeed Rich now and must so remain, I fear.'

'You have a beautiful baby, madam, and a fine home here in Essex.'

She nodded. 'And a loving family. You have met my mother and sister,

Meg, but not yet my two brothers. I hope, when Robert is older, to get him to Court. I think the Queen will enjoy him, he is a most charming and good-looking boy, so beware of him, my Meg. I think Robin will be the breaker of many hearts!'

I smiled at her words but she need not have warned me. I had met a man whom I could love, if I were older, and more intelligent, and better bred. Richard Villier seemed, to my young mind, a most perfect gentleman and I knew, even then, that he was the only person who would ever stir my heart. But, like Lady Penelope and her 'Astrophil', we were not for each other. Master Villier would have the choice of numerous beautiful ladies, with excellent dowries, and would find a bride for himself ere long, I had no doubt.

As for me, I was fortunate in having found a position with Lady Penelope Rich. I was growing ever more fond of my loving and lively mistress, and was determined to stay with her and look after her, for as long as she would have me.

Once we were back in Essex I saw dear Kate again, and the Tredworthys, and Lady Penelope was kind and allowed me free time to go to the stables and see my old friends. They wanted to know everything about Court life, and the Queen, and I had to go across and see them several times in order to tell them all they wanted to know.

'You are happy, darling?' asked Kate, gazing at me with searching eyes.

'I am completely happy,' I said, and hugged her. 'Now that my lady has one baby, and will no doubt be producing many more, we will be coming to Leighs Priory more frequently.'

'I have missed you, Meg, and thought often about you these past months. But do you mean that Lady Rich will shortly be leaving us again? How can she go to Court when her home is here?'

'My lady is not happy here,' I said softly, 'and if you were to see the gaiety of Court life you would understand, Kate. My lady is not meant for household tasks and a Puritan existence. She sings like an angel, she can play the flute, and she is an excellent dancer. How can she be happy living with a man who is against everything she most enjoys?'

'But he is her husband,' said Kate stoutly.

'And she will endeavour to give him the son and heir he desires, as well as making sure that his house is organised properly. Why, only this morning she was going through the household accounts with the steward, and checking on the stores supply. She is an excellent manager, Kate, and all will be set in perfect order before Lady Penelope goes away again.'

Kate looked at me with her black brows raised in astonishment.

'My little Margaret is no longer a child,' she said. 'You talk like a grown woman now, darling, and such know-ledge! Is that Lady Rich's influence, or from Queen Elizabeth, herself?'

I laughed. 'Indeed, not the Queen! I have seen her but at a distance and have never spoken with her. But I am learning all the time, Kate. Watching and observing and yes, my lady is a most devoted mistress and shares ideas and thoughts with me often, so it is no wonder that I am more knowledgeable than when we were last together.'

I have also learned much from a travelled and educated man, I thought. But such words were to be enfolded in my bosom and spoken aloud to no one, not even my dear Kate.

'And what of Lady Rich's mother? Do you like her?'

The Countess of Leicester had been delighted with her granddaughter, named after her, and had spent some time visiting Leighs Priory after the birth. She could not see Lady Penelope when she was at Court, so the mother came to Essex where they could spend time in each other's company.

'I feel sorry for the lady,' I told Kate, in answer to her question, 'for she does not see much of her husband. But apart from sympathy, I cannot find any liking in my heart for the Earl of Leicester's wife.'

My mistress had inherited her mother's good looks, they were indeed a striking family, for the second daughter, Dorothy, was also lovely. But whereas both the girls possessed a sparkle and a warmth, which was most attractive, Lettice, Countess of Leicester, appeared a haughty, ambitious woman to me, with little of the kindness which was apparent in her daughters.

Although my Lady Penelope was very fond of her mother, I wondered, even in those early years, whether Lettice hoped to use her children's influence in getting back to Court.

Dorothy, too, was now a maid of honour to the Queen, and it must have been tantalising for the Countess to know that both her girls, and her husband, were welcome at Court whilst she remained banished in the depths of the countryside.

I believe she had hopes that her son, Robert, on whom she doted, would eventually make his way to Court.

'And then,' I heard her say one day to Lady Penelope, 'then my sweet Robin will so charm Elizabeth that he will force her to accept me again.'

Dorothy, I liked far better than her mother, and she looked very like her sister with the same fair hair and brown eyes. Although I had heard the Earl of Leicester speaking to my lady about a possible marriage between Dorothy and Sir Philip Sidney, this was not to be. And probably just as well for the sakes of Astrophil and Stella. The following year, 1583, they were both married — but not to each other.

4

Sir Philip Sidney married Frances Walsingham, daughter of the Queen's principal secretary, and Dorothy married Tom Perrot.

The Queen took offence at the first ceremony because she had not been duly informed about it, but as neither Sir Philip nor Frances were particular favourites of hers, she remained displeased but not furious. With the marriage of Dorothy Devereux and Tom Perrot it was a very different matter, and the affair was to be the main topic of gossip at Court for many a week that summer.

The Queen's anger stemmed mainly from the fact that Dorothy was a maid of honour, and that she was the daughter of a woman whom the Queen called a she-wolf. She had hated Lettice Devereux ever since she had stolen the

Earl of Leicester, and Her Majesty was never going to forgive her for that.

My Lady Penelope's marriage had been much discussed, and all the arrangements for it had been made with the Queen's consent, so that was allowed. But Dorothy Devereux did the unforgivable — she eloped with the man of her choice without her family, or his, knowing about her plans, and she did not ask permission from the Queen, which was the worst fault of all.

The only person to know of Dorothy's wedding beforehand was Lady Penelope. She took me into her confidence one evening when we were back in Essex, after having spent a few pleasurable months at Court.

I, like my mistress, had begun dreading our return to Leighs Priory, although I enjoyed seeing Kate again and my lady, of course, could never stay away for too long because she missed little Lettice. Apart from these two reasons, I would have been quite happy to have spent all our time at Court.

I liked dressing my lady in her sumptuous gowns, and arranging her wonderful golden hair in elaborate styles, both of which were frowned upon by Lord Rich, and I always hoped to see Richard Villier, although he was not at Court so often these days.

Time spent at Leighs Priory, in contrast to Court life, was slow, and laden with pious talk and nightly catechising, and it very soon became clear to me that my lady's husband was a bully.

Once I had prepared her for bed, and brushed out her thick, long tresses which looked like molten gold in the candle-light, I would leave the chamber and return to a corner in the adjoining room where I had my truckle-bed.

Sometimes Lord Rich would be away from home, for he had been made a Justice of the Peace, being such a great landowner in Essex, and he would sit on the bench at Quarter Sessions, and at the Assize Courts. At these times both my lady and I rejoiced, and I would be called to share the huge feather-bed with her, and we would talk and giggle together like children, before falling into blissful and uninterrupted sleep.

But on the nights when Lord Rich was at Leighs Priory, I would often have to put my fingers into my ears to try and dim the frightening and abusive sounds which came from the big chamber.

He would shout at my lady, and I know he hit her many times. Not that Lady Penelope ever breathed a word of such cruelty to me, but I saw the bruises on her lovely white skin when I washed her, and I knew.

'A wife must obey the commandments of the Apostle,' I heard, shouted through the open doorway, 'who biddeth women to be silent and to learn of their husbands at home!'

Then came the thumps and the heavy breathing, and the stinging slaps of a hand on naked flesh.

'A wife must submit to all things and

be ever obedient to her husband.'

Thud, thud, slap, thump.

I clutched the blanket up over my ears, curling myself into a tight ball of hate.

How *could* he behave in such animal fashion? And he, who believed himself to be a man of God, and more righteous than most. Wicked brute! I found myself hating him more and more — his small, strutting, black-clad figure, his dark, ugly countenance, and his hard, unsmiling eyes.

A wife never quarrelled; never took strong drink, or swore; a wife was a good housekeeper, and was merry when her husband was merry, and sad when he was sad. A wife looked after her house and never left it when her husband was away from home.

If Kate had but known it, I was learning from Lord Rich, also. But learning all that I would never do, or be, in life, and the thought of marriage became more and more unacceptable in my mind.

Like Lady Penelope, I could not wait to leave Leighs Priory at the earliest possible moment, and was always overjoyed when she announced that it was time we went away again.

That evening, therefore, when I first heard about her sister's marriage plans, I was delighted to know that we would shortly be leaving Essex again. But not for Court this time, for Broxbourne, in the adjoining county of Hertfordshire.

'My dearest Dorothy has learned from my unhappy marriage that it is far, far better to choose a husband for herself,' my lady said to me, her face unusually sober in the candle-light. 'The arrangements of one's friends and family are not to be trusted, and I am the only person to know of her plans, Meg.'

I stared in silence, feeling excitement well up within my breast.

'The Queen is not going to be consulted and I fear for such action on Dorothy's part. But she is quite determined, and I like Tom Perrot and believe he will be a good and kind husband to her. They both have my blessing, and we will go to their wedding tomorrow, Meg, for they will need support and encouragement on the course they are taking.'

On the 17th July, Thomas Perrot and Dorothy Devereux took out a marriage licence issued by the Bishop of London, and they eloped to Broxbourne.

What an event that was, to be sure!

Lady Penelope and I met the small wedding party at the local church, and when the Perrot family minister asked the vicar for the keys he was refused them. However, two gentlemen of the party broke into the church and then guarded the door with swords and daggers under their cloaks, whilst the marriage took place.

Lady Penelope was flushed and exuberant, kissing her sister and new brother-in-law most heartedly after the ceremony, her black eyes sparkling with excitement. I thought she looked more beautiful than the bride, her sister, for she was wearing one of her favourite gowns — forbidden at Leighs Priory — of dark blue satin, over a dress of pale blue silk. The gown was tightly-waisted and then fell open, showing the embroidered dress beneath, which was covered with sprigs of tiny flowers all sewn with pearls. Her quilted sleeves were dark blue, also decorated with pearls, and on her golden hair was a fine, jewelled head-dress with a long, transparent veil behind, falling to below her shoulders.

The day ended less happily, unfortunately, for the angry relatives arrived some hours later and poor Tom Perrot and the minister were taken away and imprisoned in Fleet Prison.

Dorothy, too, suffered, for the Queen was so furious that she banished Dorothy from Court, just like her mother. Unbelievably, my Lady Penelope remained unharmed by this event, and was allowed to continue with her attendance on the Queen as if nothing untoward had happened.

'I am lucky, Meg,' she told me, when we were safely back at Court, 'I have a feeling that Fate will always smile on me. Perhaps because I was once named Stella? Thus remaining a star, shining brightly and never allowed to dim by bad luck.'

'I hope so, madam,' I answered quietly. 'Your luck is certainly riding high at present, especially at Court.'

I did not think that anyone could call her marriage to Lord Rich a matter of good fortune, but so long as she stayed in favour with the Queen nothing too terrible could harm her.

And what splendid days those were for us, at Court, constantly filled with excitement and pageantry. I remember telling Kate of the Accession Day Tilts that year, held at Whitehall on the 17th November.

This day was always most memorable, and especially thrilling for the London crowds who were allowed to enter the stands if they could find the sum of twelve pence.

At midday the Queen and her ladies placed themselves at windows in a long room of the Palace, overlooking the tilt-yard. From this room a staircase led downwards, and at the foot of this all the knights who were taking part in the tournament, would stop and greet Her Majesty. Then a servant would mount the steps and address the Queen with words of a verse, and in the name of his lord present her with a pageant shield, which was the painted device his knight would wear in combat.

The knights had their servants clad in different colours, and their horses, too, were of extraordinary fashions. I saw one horse dressed like an elephant, which caused much amusement, and the knights themselves were attired in strange and unusual ways. Some of their disguises were romantic, some comic, and I remember seeing an Enchanted Knight, and a Black Knight, and a Clownish Knight, amongst others.

I told Kate of the many painted

devices, and the beauty of some, with the Queen often depicted as an astral body. There were sheep painted on them, and clouds, and one with an eye weeping onto a heart. There were roses, and dragons, and a phoenix arising out of golden flames. They all meant something special, symbolic to each different knight, and I was awed by such cleverness and wit; understanding nothing, but revelling in the pageantry of everything I saw.

The armours worn were equally impressive, gilded with hearts and vine leaves, true lovers' knots and roses.

Within the tilt-yard was a pavilion where the judges sat and, attended by heralds, they took down the scores. In the centre of the surrounding stands was the tilt-rail and the knights approached it, two at a time, from opposite ends of the lists, and rode fiercely at each other, endeavouring to shatter each others' lances.

I never tired of watching the Accession Day Tilts, and always managed to find a good viewing point with Annie. Our ladies, meanwhile, were in fine positions, attending the Queen high above our heads at the Palace windows.

Sir Philip Sidney married his Frances in September of that year, so the days of Astrophil and Stella were well and truly over, and the following year, 1584, I met Robert Devereux, the young Earl of Essex, for the first time.

Lady Penelope had been at Leighs Priory for several weeks that spring, and as the time spent there had been more than usually fraught with arguments and bad temper, she suddenly decided that it was time she visited Chartley Manor, her old home.

'It is lovely there, Meg, and Mother lives nearby when she is not at Wanstead, waiting for Leicester to return, so we will go to Staffordshire and visit both her and my brother.'

I was not so pleased at the thought of seeing Lettice again, but a meeting with Robert Devereux intrigued me. I was also thankful to be getting away from

Lord Rich's aggressive voice and belligerent behaviour for a while. Not that I saw much of him or, indeed, was ever in his company for long. My poor lady had to bear the brunt of his brutish manners. But I suffered mentally whenever Lady Penelope was with him, and it was a great joy to know that we would soon be in a more harmonious atmosphere.

Chartley Manor was a few miles north-west of Stafford, with the Needwood Forest stretching away to the east. It was a beautiful moated house, half-timbered, with gables, tall chimneys and many windows. I loved the place as soon as I saw it, and understood why my lady had wished to revisit her childhood home. There were close on one thousand acres of land, she told me proudly, and the Chartley cattle were a famous and unique breed with their long, branching horns.

I was less impressed with the young earl. He was handsome, of that there was no doubt, with the same striking good looks as his mother and sisters. Essex had dark eyes, also, but his hair was a rich red-brown, and he was very self-assured, very mature, for a lad of but seventeen years. He was tall and slender, with well-muscled legs, but possessed an arrogance which offended me. His mother obviously adored him, and seemed to spend more time with him at Chartley, than she did in her own home at Drayton Bassett.

My lady, too, doted on her young brother so it was little wonder that he should possess a very high opinion of himself.

There was much revelry during our days at Chartley, and such singing and dancing that I did not think I had ever seen Lady Penelope looking so well and happy.

During one of the banquets in the Great Hall, which I was watching from the gallery above, I felt a hand touch my shoulder and turned to find Richard Villier standing beside me.

'You!' I cried out, astonished and

thrilled to see his good face again.

'Indeed, me,' he answered, his mouth curling with a smile, and his green eyes fairly sparkling into mine.

'I am so surprised.' I lowered my head, trying to conceal the blood which was burning up my neck, suffusing my cheeks in a tell-tale stain of emotion. 'I have not seen you for many a month, sir, and believed you to have left Court for good.'

'But this is not Court, Meg, and my home is in Shropshire, if you remember?'

I nodded.

'As I know young Essex and wished to purchase some cattle from him, I took it upon myself to come up here and spend a few days in jovial company.'

'Jovial it is.' I looked away from his searching gaze and viewed the crowded hall below.

'Do you like to dance, Meg? I have never asked before because it was not possible at Court. But here, in such informal surroundings, a dance with you would not be frowned upon, and the Queen is safely at Whitehall.'

My blush deepened and I shook my head vigorously. 'I cannot dance, sir. At least, only around the Maypole.'

'Then come down with me and take your chance with a galliard. You must have seen the Queen performing it, and your Lady Penelope dances it almost nightly at Court. You cannot tell me that you do not know what to do with your feet, Meg.'

He was so determined, his eyes brimming with such infectious delight, that I could not refuse him and down I went, on Richard Villier's arm, deciding to do my very best and hoping that my lady would not see me and laugh at my mistakes.

My companion was wearing a doublet of grey silk over which hung a sleeveless jerkin of black velvet; his Venetians were a deep rose in colour, and fastened by pearl buttons at his knees. On his fine legs were stockings of pink silk, embroidered with silver thread.

I had felt quite elegant in my gown of jade green, over a primrose under-dress, with lace at my wrists, and a small ruff which my lady, in her generosity, had allowed me to wear. In fact, the gown and dress were both hers, thrown out as she was continually purchasing new garments, and I was gradually filling a chest of my own.

But I lacked jewels, which I saw on all the ladies of fashion, and wished that I could have been more sumptuously attired beside my handsome partner. My brown hair was not puffed out, nor crimped, but caught in a heavy knot at the back of my head. However, Master Villier looked at me with admiration, apparently noticing none of my defects, so I was well pleased.

I must confess that I was not pleased with my dancing at first, feeling ashamed of my clodhopping feet. But Richard Villier was a wonderful and patient partner, and I learned the galliard that evening so that I would never fear it again.

Later, as I saw that Lady Penelope was busy at the card-tables, and would not be needing my assistance for some time to come, I obeyed my companion's demands and walked with him in the long gallery which overlooked the moat.

'You have asked me much about myself, Meg, and I have told you of my past history, yet I know little about you,' remarked Richard, placing my hand over his arm and walking sedately with me down the wooden boards. 'Tell me, who were your parents, and where were you born?'

'My father's name was Henry Dawlish, and my mother died when I was born. We lived in a house above a shop in Cheapside during the first years of my life, and Father was a merchant of cloth.'

'Go on.'

'There is little more to say about that early period, save that Father married again and Kate and I were not happy. When he died, Kate took me to her sister in Essex.'

'Who was Kate?'

'Kate is my only family, not by blood but by loving. She has looked after me ever since my mother died.'

Richard Villier pondered a moment. Then,

'What happened to the shop?' he asked. 'Did you inherit nothing on your father's death? You were the only child, I presume? No brothers or sisters?'

I shook my head. 'I suppose Mistress Gwendoline took over the shop. She certainly brought in new servants when Father died. I wonder if it is still there in Cheapside. Do you know, sir?'

'I do not, but will take a look next time I am in the City of London. Why were you and Kate not happy, Meg?'

His question brought back memories which had lain dormant at the back of my mind for many years. So much had happened to me since our flight from London, that I had forgotten Kate's fear for me and the urgency of our departure.

'I know that Mistress Gwendoline was not kind to us,' I replied slowly, 'and both Kate and I were expected to keep out of sight once Father died. I must ask Kate about it when we return to Leighs Priory, but I remember her saying that we had to run away, and that she feared danger. Once we left Cheapside there was so much to see, and so many new things to think about, we never spoke about the past again.'

'I wonder.' Richard's face had become very thoughtful. 'It seems to me that you should have inherited some of your father's possessions, if not all of them. Maybe the new wife was jealous of you and what you would receive from the will, so Kate ran away with you in case there was an attempt on your life. Could be, you know. And now a very wealthy Gwendoline is sitting in Cheapside owning part, or all, of your rightful inheritance.'

'Goodness me, that cannot be true!' I

slowed my steps and looked up at him. 'Do not tell me that I should be a wealthy young woman now! Not after all these years as a laundry woman, and living with hoards of children in a small room above the stables. I cannot believe that, Richard Villier!'

'Why not? Worse things have happened to people who should have inherited much. Kate might well have saved your life, but she did not do you any further justice. It would have been more sensible if she had gone to a lawyer and begged for help. No doubt you were pronounced dead, after you vanished, and thus everything was passed into Mistress Gwendoline's avaricious hands.'

'She did like beautiful jewels and fine clothes,' I said, 'I remember how she looked, and how she dressed, quite well.'

'Then I shall endeavour to find out the truth for you, Margaret Dawlish, and, who knows, you may yet find yourself an heiress with young men running around you anxious to receive your hand in marriage, and your dowry.'

I smiled, determined not to blush again.

'From what I have seen of marriage it is not for me, sir, and besides, Kate's flight took me to Essex and there I met Lady Penelope Rich.' I looked straight at him, any confusion gone from my mind. 'Truly, I have never been happier than these last two years in her company. Nobody could ask for a kinder mistress, or a better life than the one I have now.'

'But think of the future, Meg. You cannot want to serve Lady Rich for the rest of your days?'

'I shall stay with her for as long as she wants me,' I replied quietly. 'And if that means to the end of her life, or of mine, I shall remain.'

'What nonsense you talk.' His eyes had lost their merriment and he looked quite fierce. 'You are very young, Meg, and this life suits you at present, for which I am glad. But to see you as an ageing servant, hobbling after an even older mistress, is absurd! You must want children one day, and a house to call your own?'

'Neither tempt me, sir.'

I was seeing houses, beautiful homes, all the time; Leighs Priory, the Palace of Whitehall, this gracious Chartley Manor. I was having my fill of places but desired none of them. Like my lady, I enjoyed a few weeks here, a few weeks there, but was always pleased to be on the move again after a while.

As for children, I had lived for too long amidst the ever-growing Tredworthy family to relish the thought of feeding, washing, and clothing innumerable babies. As it was, Lady Penelope was expecting another one and we would soon have to return to Essex, to await the arrival of the second Rich. I had also seen what my lady had to endure in order to produce offspring for her husband, and I was not prepared to go through such nightly disturbances in the bedchamber.

'No,' I shook my head. 'I think not, Master Villier. Possessions are a nuisance and, indeed, I want for nothing. My lady is most generous towards me and I have only to ask for a new gown and she will at once produce one for me. I desire nothing more from life, I do assure you.'

He removed my hand from his arm and placed both his firmly upon my shoulders.

'Sometimes, Meg Dawlish,' he said, 'I could dearly throttle you.'

Then his hands lifted to my face and he tilted my head backwards and bent forward to kiss me hard on the mouth.

This was my first proper embrace. Of course, my father had petted and kissed me, and I had been cuddled by both Kate and my Lady Penelope. But I had never received the demanding, warm lips of a man before, and the emotion which Richard Villier aroused within me was frightening.

Suddenly, and quite unexpectedly, I

realised what desire meant, and for a brief moment I wanted to hold and be held, to experience all the lusts of the flesh, to relax totally and allow this man to do with me what he would.

Then Richard pulled back, lifting his face from mine, and the humour had returned to his eyes as he looked down at me, although there was tenderness as well as amusement in them.

'You are not made to be a virgin, my dear Meg,' he said huskily, stroking my cheek with one hand. 'You were made for loving, and I fear that all the proud thoughts about your future will be thwarted. Hopefully, by me.'

I caught my breath and stepped away from him, annoyed with myself for giving in so easily to his embrace. So this was how they felt, those girls who produced babies before they were wed, and whom I had always scorned. Was this, perhaps, how Lady Penelope felt when she eventually succumbed to her husband's violent bursts of passion? Oh, she did not love him, that I knew.

But maybe, at the last, she gave in as readily as I so easily could have done?

Richard Villier was charming, good-looking and yes, very desirable. But I would not give in and spend my years producing babies and keeping house. In that respect my Lady Penelope was fortunate; she had the wealth to make her independent, and a husband who, although he did not like it, allowed her frequent absences from home because of her favour with the Queen.

Surely there were not many females with such an opportunity, and I felt very sure that Richard Villier, for one, would expect his wife to remain at home all the time.

'No, Master Villier,' I said adamantly, 'the married state is not for me. With my lady I have freedom from all household drudgery, and lead a life which is indeed blessed. I am fortunate in having a most excellent mistress and life with her is what I enjoy above all else.'

I understood now why the Queen

had remained a virgin; she retained her independence whilst, at the same time, enjoying the company of men and indulging herself with numerous favourites and flirtations.

I liked Richard Villier; I liked being in his company and watching the admiration in his eyes. It was certain in my mind that I would never feel such affection for any other man, nor desire the companionship of any other male so much. But marriage, if that was what he intended, must always be refused, and an affair equally ignored, if such a relationship was asked of me. That was the only way in which I could keep my independence, and the happiness and excitement which I now shared with Lady Penelope Rich.

'What if Lady Rich should no longer require your assistance? What if she should die? Do not shudder at the thought and look so angry! I hope that such a tragedy will never befall you, but it is possible, Meg. Many females die in childbirth, as you must realise when remembering your own mother.'

'My lady will never cease to want my attentions.'

That much was certain. We were so akin in thoughts and ideas, even though Lady Penelope was far more intelligent and better educated than I. We had the same sense of fun, and she knew that I could be trusted and thus opened out her heart to me on many occasions, knowing that nothing she said, or did, would ever be repeated to another soul.

'If she should die, and God forbid that such a terrible thing should ever occur prematurely, then I shall have to re-plan my life, Master Villier. But until such a time, I shall remain her loving servant and be totally content.'

He shrugged, and his mouth turned down at the corners.

'If that is your will, so be it. But I shall keep watch on you, Margaret Dawlish, and there may well come a time when you could use a helping hand, or even change your mind. So remember me, and do not hesitate to call if you should need my assistance.'

'You are a good man, sir. I do not think I could ever forget you, even if I wanted to. Now, take me back to the Great Hall,' I went on hastily, as he reached for me again, 'it is time I went back to my duty and attended on my lady.'

'Stubborn wench,' muttered Richard Villier, taking my hand and linking it through his arm once more, then beginning to walk with me down the long gallery. 'A stubborn wench, with a heart of ice. But ice melts in time and I shall not give up hope of thawing the frost in you one day.'

5

In due course we returned to Leighs Priory and Lady Penelope's second daughter was born and named Essex, after her brother. Lord Rich was not the slightest bit interested in this girl-child and renewed his nightly efforts to beget a son. He owned so much land, was the possessor of so much wealth, that he had now become desperate for a son and heir.

My lady bore the misery and abuse for as long as she could, then we thankfully departed for Court once more, where our real happiness lay waiting.

The year 1585 was filled with new happenings, new experiences.

Robert Devereux, the young Earl of Essex, had been living too lavishly, using much of his inheritance in the country, so both his mother and my lady were delighted when he made his way to Court. Essex was so assured, so handsome and young, that the Queen was enchanted with him, and his family breathed a sigh of relief and hoped that he would soon gain favours, in order to replenish his emptying coffers.

During that year my lady was painted by Master Nicholas Hilliard and I, too, was painted by him, which was one of the proudest moments of my life. This talented and great artist, who was continually making portraits of the Queen and other less important but nonetheless influential people, this man, asked Lady Penelope if I could be spared the time to sit for him.

She readily agreed, being the loving and generous person she was, and although Master Hilliard had offered to paint me free of charge because he said my face was 'interesting', Lady Penelope paid him in full for my portrait, and this helped the man greatly with his money problems.

It seemed so strange to me that some

people were unable to handle their money properly. Robert, Earl of Essex, was forever in debt and Nicholas Hilliard was also in financial difficulties most of the time.

My lady told me that Hilliard was fortunate in having a father-in-law who was a Chamberlain of the City, but Nicholas and his wife, Alice, produced many babies and were constantly in debt despite his fine portrait painting. Thus making me even more certain that I would not be trapped into marriage, myself.

However, I was delighted at the idea of being painted, and my lady and I ventured forth to Hilliard's house and workshop in Gutter Lane on several occasions, to sit for the talented man.

Lady Penelope always looked radiant and wore such splendid gowns that I knew she would be depicted beautifully. But I wanted to look beautiful, too, although Master Hilliard said that the simplicity of my attire would enhance my 'interesting' face. Fortunately, my lady gave in to my pleas and, as she was paying for the portrait, Master Hilliard obeyed her demands.

I was thus attired in a black velvet gown belonging to Lady Penelope Rich, and my throat was encircled by a laced ruff encrusted with silver, which my lady had given permission for me to wear. Normally, no servant wore a lace ruff for this was a symbol of nobility. But for my painting I wore one and occasionally, well away from Court, Lady Penelope allowed me to wear the enchanting ruff around my neck. For Master Hilliard I also wore my lady's pearls in my ears and on my tightly ringleted hair, and did not look like Margaret Dawlish at all, when the miniature was finished, but like an elegant and very pretty lady.

'I shall keep it for you, Meg,' said Lady Penelope, holding it in one of her hands and gazing down at the magnificent interpretation of me with great fondness in her eyes. 'We move around so much it must never be lost. I shall place it in my jewel-case and you have only to tell me when you want it, and I will give it to you.'

I was happy with this decision and deep inside my heart a little voice said,

'Maybe Richard Villier would like it?'

The painting of my lady was large, big enough to be framed and hung upon a wall at Leighs Priory. But mine was a miniature and Lady Penelope had it framed in an oval of gold, enamelled with blue, and with a ring attached at the top so that it could be hung from a chain.

These miniatures were made for private viewing, to be hung around the neck of the owner, and to be kept, like my lady intended, in a secret place. They were often used as love-tokens and kept as treasures to be taken out and admired when lovers were parted from each other. Later, I was to see my lady with one, not the one of me, held often in her hands, and the man she loved was also to possess one of her.

We were to see Nicholas Hilliard

frequently over the next few years, and admire more of his work when he began painting Lady Penelope's brother, Robert, and another of my lady. When one of Hilliard's daughters was born he named her Penelope, after my Lady Rich.

In this same year the Earl of Leicester departed for the Netherlands leaving his wife alone yet again. Robert Devereux, the young Earl of Essex, went with him, as did many men from Court. They went, my lady explained, to fight against the Spanish forces who were occupying the Netherlands. With both her husband and her son gone from England, the Countess of Leicester spent more time than ever with her eldest daughter, whenever my lady could drag herself away from Court.

Frances Sidney also came to see Lady Penelope to tell her that Sir Philip, too, had gone across the sea to fight for the Protestant cause against the Spanish. Frances was proud of the fact that the Queen had made her husband Governor of Flushing, but she missed him, and was fearful for his life.

So the three worried ladies joined company at Leighs Priory and encouraged each other to keep their strength up, and to forget their anxieties in the enjoyment of the little girls. My lady had Lettice and Essex, of course, and Frances Sidney also had a little daughter, named Elizabeth.

The Countess of Leicester's baby son, Lord Denbigh, which she had had by her second husband, had died the year before, so all her hopes for the future were based upon her adored son, Robert Devereux. She had another son, Walter, by her first marriage to my lady's father, but I had never met him. Both Lady Penelope and her mother seemed to idolise the young Earl of Essex, and his name was seldom off their lips whilst he was away fighting in the Netherlands.

Frances Sidney I found to be as irritating as Lettice, Countess of Leicester. When I told Richard Villier later, that I did not care for these ladies, he accused me of being jealous.

'You do not like anyone who takes Penelope Rich's affection away from you, Meg,' he said.

I could not agree with this, for I liked her sister, Dorothy, very much, although we did not see so much of her now that she was happily married, and her husband, Tom Perrot, had finally been released from Fleet Prison.

Frances Sidney was a dark-haired, quiet lady, with mournful large eyes and a soft, drooping mouth. It always puzzled me that Sir Philip could have loved her after knowing the warmth and gaiety of my Lady Penelope.

However, the main reason for my dislike of her was her enormous pride in her father, the Queen's private secretary, and his ingenuity in catching spies. She was boasting about him constantly, and I think even my lady's mother became annoyed with her.

I used to sit in a corner of the room, busy with my sewing, listening to the ladies' talk, with my ears stretched out as if on sticks. So I heard the disagreement one day, when Lettice announced that Chartley Manor had been taken over, whilst her son was away, and used as a prison for Mary Queen of Scots.

'They decided that as Chartley has a moat it would be an ideal place for her,' she snapped, and her black eyes, so like my lady's, smouldered with anger. 'It is all Walsingham's fault. He hopes to trap Mary by reading secret letters which she smuggles out of the Manor.'

'If it is Father's idea then it must be a good one,' answered Frances coldly. 'He is a remarkably clever man, and it is time that female was found guilty of treason and executed.'

Lady Penelope looked from one companion to the other but would not take part in the argument, and I wished that the Queen would either have Mary beheaded, or else banished to some far country. We were always hearing of plots and counter-plots, and how the Catholics wanted to have Mary made queen instead of Elizabeth, and there was trouble enough with Spain, as it was.

'Now they are cutting down trees on the estate, and I dare not think what condition the house and land will be in when my poor Robin returns home,' grumbled the Countess.

'He will be thankful to have helped the Queen,' answered Frances smoothly, 'and no doubt my father will be justly rewarded if his plan works.'

Some while later, when we were alone together, my lady informed me that Walsingham's plan had borne fruit, and that Mary would soon be removed to Fotheringay Castle.

'At least they will then leave poor Chartley alone,' she said.

'How did Walsingham succeed?' I asked.

'He gained the support of Ned Fields, who always supplies Chartley with ale. Mary was smuggling letters out of the manor inside the barrels, in waterproof containers, and Anthony

Babington was sending her notes in the same way. They both believed it was entirely safe, not knowing that Walsingham's men were reading everything.'

'What will happen to the Queen of Scots now?'

Lady Penelope shrugged. 'Everyone of importance is begging the Queen to have Mary beheaded, in order to safeguard herself, and this entire country, against the might of Spain.'

I did not have strong feelings against the Catholics, indeed, I was not sure that Puritanism was not worse, if Lord Rich were a prime example of it. But then politics were not of great interest to me, and I could not understand why so many men had to leave England and go to fight in another country for political, or religious, reasons. It seemed so senseless to my unintelligent mind.

But when I ventured such views to Kate, she told me that the Catholics would kill anyone who did not believe as they did. She said it was far safer for us to live in a Protestant country, under the good Protestant Queen Bess.

'The Spanish are devils, Meg,' she ended fiercely, 'I remember your dear father telling me that so often, and they believe that theirs is the only true religion. We haven't heard the last of them yet, you mark my words. Once they have finished their evil work on the continent, they will be coming over here, and that will mean the death of you, and me, and everyone who is not a Catholic.'

Her words frightened me, and I felt very glad that there was a wide expanse of water between our countries, and that England was a safe little island.

That autumn there was tragic news from the Netherlands. At the end of September a small group of horsemen thundered into the courtyard at Leighs Priory and, looking from an upstairs window, I saw that they were led by Richard Villier.

When he entered the chamber in which we women were grouped, I saw his mud-stained, weary body advance slowly towards Frances Sidney.

'Bad news, my lady,' he said, bowing before her. 'Your husband has been wounded at the battle of Zutphen, and if you wish to see him again, I would urge you to travel with me tomorrow.'

'Robin!' screamed the Countess of Leicester, rising to her feet with both hands clutched to her bosom. 'Is Robin alive?'

How typical of the lady to ask after her dear son before mentioning her husband's name, I thought. But my eyes were on Lady Penelope, and I wondered how she would feel hearing the bad news about the man she had once loved.

Penelope Rich looked as white as parchment, as did Frances Sidney, but my lady had risen at once and moved across to her friend, all her thoughts for this woman who was suffering the most.

'Dearest Frances,' said my lady, bending over her, 'do not despair. Go with Master Villier tomorrow, if that is what you desire, and travel to Philip's side as swiftly as possible.'

'I want to go — I must see him again,' whispered Frances, clinging to Lady Penelope's outstretched hands.

For once I felt great compassion for Frances Sidney in her wretched plight.

'What happened?' she asked Richard, lifting her huge brown eyes and gazing at him with dread. 'Tell me what happened.'

Richard raised a hand to his tired face and rubbed it before saying hoarsely,

'Leicester and Sidney had five hundred and fifty men in all, to face a Spanish convoy of some three thousand foot soldiers and well over one thousand cavalry. It was madness, all of it, but they would not retreat.

'Your husband, madam, had armed himself fully, but when he noticed that the Marshal of the Camp was only partially armed, he removed his own thigh-pieces. It was this chivalrous behaviour which was his undoing, for he was wounded in the thigh.'

'Will he not recover?'

'Philip is dying, madam,' said Richard gently.

There was complete silence in the room for a moment, broken only by a shuddering sigh from Frances, and then the slow, painful sound of her muffled sobs. We were all remembering the handsome courtly gentleman, with his unbreakable code of honour, his beautiful writing, and his wit and intelligence.

'Whilst he was lying wounded he called for a drink,' Richard went on speaking quietly, 'and as he was putting the bottle to his mouth he saw a young soldier, also badly wounded, who was carried past him. This young lad was looking at the bottle in such a way that Philip knew he was crazed with thirst. So he lowered the bottle from his own mouth and held it out to the poor soldier, saying, 'Your need is greater than mine'.'

After Richard had spoken those

words his head sank to his chest, but not before I had seen the gleam of moisture on his cheeks.

It was the only time I ever saw Richard Villier weep.

Francis Sidney and my lady remained silent, but the Countess took a deep breath.

'Is Robin all right?' she asked again.

Richard lifted his head and braced back his shoulders. 'Yes, my lady,' he replied. 'Your son is safe and well, and showed great bravery on the field. He shattered his lance on the first Spaniard he met, but rode on at the head of his troop, hacking his way with an axe. There was great bravery to be seen, and much chivalry.' he added, 'it is only sad that so many men had to give up their lives on that day.'

Frances Sidney left with Richard the following morning, leaving her baby, Elizabeth, in our safe-keeping. She arrived in time to see her husband before he died on the 17th October.

Sir Philip Sidney chose as his heir for

the role of champion of the Protestant cause, the brother of the woman he had once loved — Robert, Earl of Essex, and he bequeathed him his best sword.

Both my lady and I were glad when that year ended, and we would have taken ourselves thankfully back to Court, but for the fact that Lady Penelope was expecting another child.

The Countess of Leicester removed herself to Wanstead to meet her husband on his return from the Netherlands, and she also saw her beloved Robin there, for it was easier for her to see him so near to Court, rather than if she buried herself in the Staffordshire countryside.

Sir Philip's widow left us also, to return to Walsingham House so we were on our own again, apart from the dubious companionship of Lord Rich. My lady missed the dancing and singing which she loved so much, but when Lord Rich was away from home, she would take out her lute and play most beautifully for me.

We heard news of the world outside at various times that spring, brought to us by Richard Villier. My lady appeared to like him, and his presence was tolerated by her husband because he came from Court, and was always very correct in his manner towards Lord Rich.

In such a restricted and puritanical household it was not possible for us to meet and talk privately, but I was always present when he called on Lady Penelope, and I knew when he smiled and greeted her that his thoughts were really on me.

Thus we heard of Mary Queen of Scots' execution on the 8th February, and of Sir Philip Sidney's funeral at St Paul's Cathedral on the 16th of the same month.

'If it please you,' said Richard, looking straight at my lady, 'there were stars engraved on the gloves, and on the helmet of his armour.' Lord Rich was not present at that time so Richard could speak his mind. 'And a pennant from his battle array, which was carried in the funeral procession, showed a fish looking up at the stars with the motto — 'Beauty for its own sake'.'

'So he did not forget me, even at the last, even with Frances,' said my lady.

'No, madam, he never forgot you and his poetry will live forever.'

'You know about mine?' she said in some surprise. 'I thought they were written for me, nobody else.'

'A few good friends were also allowed to read and enjoy 'Astrophil and Stella', and I hope that one day they may be published so that the whole world can enjoy them. Philip was a very fine poet, my lady, and those were amongst his best.'

'He was a very fine man,' she replied softly, 'the worthiest knight that ever lived.'

To everyone's joy and delight Lady Rich produced a son that March, and this, her third child, was named Robert. Lord Rich fondly believed that the boy was named after him, but both my lady and I knew that he was named after her adored brother, Robert, the Earl of Essex.

Once she had done her duty and recovered in health, my lady returned to Court and I, most thankfully, went with her. It was so good to get back to the gaiety and the gossip, and the sheer enjoyment of living, after too long in the austere atmosphere of Leighs Priory.

Annie was pleased to see me again and she brought me up to date on all the chat and intrigue, which had been so lacking in my life during the past months.

'There is a new young man who has caught the Queen's eye,' she told me, at the first opportunity we had to get together, whilst our ladies were attending on Her Majesty. 'His name is Charles Blount and I fear that Essex is not best pleased.'

'Tell me more,' I said, laughing at my friend's knowing expression.

'He is twenty-four years old and

comes from an ancient and noble family whose fortunes have been depleted. His home is at Canford Manor in Dorset, but he is most often at Court these days.'

'Handsome?' I asked, though surely he must be, for the Queen most favoured the physically attractive men.

'Most handsome,' answered Annie, 'but he is not flirtatious and has many ladies crying alone in their beds at night because of his lack of interest.'

'What does he look like?'

'You will see him soon, I have no doubt, but rest assured that Charles Blount is tall, with dark hair and beautiful brown eyes. He possesses a most cheerful and amiable face, and eats and drinks the very best foods and wines, but never in excess.'

He sounded to me somewhat like Sir Philip Sidney, and I wondered. Would this virtuous and modest young man find my lady attractive? And, if so, would she, after the sorrow of losing Sir Philip, want the love and affection of another man? Especially if he was a favourite of the Queen?

I did not have long to ponder. Within a few days I could see that Lady Penelope was glowing with happiness, and although she always looked radiant when she was away from Leighs Priory, this was different.

'I am in love again, Meg,' she told me, as I was dressing her for a banquet to be held at the Palace that night. 'I thought that I would never feel passion again, but it has happened to me after five long years, and I believe he feels the same.'

She spun round in her gown of scarlet satin, which was embroidered all over with pearls. Tiny circlets of them studded her bodice, and her skirts, and a single plumed fan was attached to a long gold chain around her waist which hung almost to the floor. Her over-sleeves were scarlet, slashed with gold, and on her puffed-out hair I had fixed a cap of gold cloth, encrusted with pearls.

My lady's eyes shone like the stars

she had been named after; black, glittering, marvellous eyes. No man in his senses could resist them.

'Of course he will feel the same for you, my lady. And this gown is perfect for tonight.' I fastened a gold chain around her neck, beneath the ruff, from which hung a ruby cut into the shape of a heart.

'His name is Charles Blount, Meg, and he is such a quiet, gentle man I feel that I could spend the rest of my days with him in complete tranquillity.'

I looked at her. 'What about Lord Rich?'

She nodded, her face becoming sober. 'That is my misfortune, is it not? What was it Philip said? Can you remember those words — 'But that rich fool, who by blind Fortune's lot the richest gem of love and life enjoys, and can with foul abuse such beauties blot'. Well, my beauty shall not be blotted by my Rich husband, try as he will. I shall come to Court as often as I can, and I shall love, Meg, love a really good man once again. Why should I die without knowing true happiness?'

'What if Lord Rich should find out?'

I had been worried enough during those early meetings with Sir Philip Sidney, how much harder would it be to protect my lady now? She was several years married, she was the mother of three children, and one was now heir to the Rich fortune.

'Oh, my lady, take care,' I cried. 'He will punish you most dreadfully if he discovers you with another man.'

'I think not.' Lady Penelope placed pearls in her ears and two ruby rings upon her long fingers. 'I believe that I am too useful to my husband here at Court, and can often make deals for him, and write letters to appropriate people for him, using my name. We Devereuxs are still in power here, Meg, despite the Queen's hatred of my mother. And so long as the Earl of Leicester carries on in favour, and my brother, Robert, preens himself in readiness for the eventual take-over, I do not think that anything will be denied me. I can therefore assist my husband in many different ways, and he knows it.'

My lady was also greatly pleased when the Queen bestowed the post of Master of Horse upon her brother in the June of that year.

'Such a position is worth £1,500 each year, Meg,' she told me, 'as well as all the free stabling and the jousting entertainments that will go with it. Her Majesty is most pleased with our dearest Robin, as Mother always believed she would be.'

'But your mother, the Countess, may still not return to Court?' I asked. 'Even with her son in such good grace?'

'No.' Lady Penelope shook her fair head. 'Mother is banished the same as ever.'

6

Being at Court again for some length of time enabled me to see Richard Villier again, and talk with him properly as I had been unable to do for many months. My lady, I think, had guessed at Richard's feelings towards me and, because she knew what it was like to love and yet have many obstacles in one's path, she allowed me considerable freedom, often saying that she would be involved in attendance on the Queen until such and such a time, and giving me several hours in which to do exactly what I liked.

Of course, I liked to spend time with Richard Villier, and whenever he was able we would meet in an empty chamber on the second floor, overlooking the stable-yard.

'Well, Meg,' he told me one afternoon, 'I have been to see your father's old shop in Cheapside and noticed how well Mistress Gwendoline is doing for herself.' He looked most dashing in his brown doublet, with padded sleeves of ruby red slashed with gold. He wore trunk hose of deep brown velvet, and his stockings of red silk were embroidered with gold thread. 'Did you speak to Kate Haddock about your father's will when you were in Essex?'

'I did not. There were so many other things on my mind I quite forgot. But as I told you before, Master Villier, I really am not interested in the past. The present is so very interesting; who cares what should, or should not, have happened all those years ago?'

'Still stubborn and, if I dare say it, stupid,' he remarked shortly.

'I am not stupid!' I turned on him, angered by his scornful words. 'I know that I do not possess half the wit and intelligence of my mistress, but I do have a brain, sir, and am quite able to think for myself without your assistance. I do not *want* more money. I am entirely satisfied with my life today and neither a dowry, nor half-ownership of that shop, would interest me in the smallest way!'

I was almost at the door before he stopped me. I enjoyed his company and wanted to hear him talk about Court life and what was going on there, expressed from a man's point of view. I did *not* want commands on what to do with my life and how I should try to improve it.

'If you are not careful you will become as belligerent and as bullying as odious Lord Rich!' I cried, as his fingers clasped around my wrist and he dragged me back into his strong arms.

'In some ways I wish I was like him,' he muttered, rubbing his face in my hair and holding me so close that I could feel his heart pounding beneath his doublet. 'I would like to get you to bed, Margaret Dawlish, and beat your soft white flesh until you cried out for mercy.'

'Brute!'

I could say no more, for his mouth closed on mine and all words were silenced. His hands moved over my body, smoothing the velvet above my breasts, stroking and caressing my neck and the skin above my tightly-laced bodice.

'I want to see you naked, Meg,' he breathed, lifting his face a few inches from mine and then bending his head to place warm, nibbling kisses on my trembling shoulders. 'Are you half so lovely as you appear? So warmly clad, so unreachable, so damned desirable!'

'Enough!' I pushed him away from me and stepped back, pulling the velvet more firmly up to my shoulders and rearranging the crumpled lace at my breast. 'Such behaviour is dangerous, and I do not wish to stay here if you fondle me so provocatively. Let us talk, but talk calmly, and leave a space between us. Otherwise I shall take my leave of you, be assured of that.'

Richard Villier sighed and gazed down at me with sombre eyes. 'I may not call you stupid, but I repeat that you are a stubborn wench. I cannot understand such modesty. Why, half the maids at Court are rejoicing nightly with their lovers, and the other half are green with envy, wishing that they were doing likewise.'

'You underrate the female sex, sir,' I said indignantly. 'The Queen is a perfect example of feminine charm linked with virginity, and all the young maids admire her and are proud to follow suit.'

Richard shook his head. 'They follow their mistresses' examples, not the Queen's, and I wait to see how long it will be before you follow your Lady Rich to some man's bed.'

'That is wicked talk, sir, and I will not listen! My lady was forced into a marriage she did not want, but since then she has been an admirable wife and produced three healthy babies, including a son and heir, and these for a husband she dislikes,' I snapped.

'There was Philip,' he went on,

ignoring my outburst, 'and now Sir Charles is being hunted, I can see it plainly.'

'*Sir* Charles?'

'Blount has just been knighted by Leicester for his services in the Netherlands, and the Queen has made him Keeper of the New Forest to help him support himself. Oh, your Lady Penelope does not give her affection to mere nobodies, Meg, you must have noticed that?'

'She is a most warm and generous lady, and if Sir Charles Blount is half as nice as she is, he will be fortunate in receiving her attention,' I said defiantly.

'Then I hope she will be careful,' answered Richard, 'for I can see in Blount the same kind of courage and chivalry and intelligence as Philip possessed. Those qualities did not help Sir Philip Sidney when his life was cut off at the age of thirty-two, so let us pray that Sir Charles Blount fares better. But I fear that Penelope Rich carries bad luck with her, like some black cloud, and I would not want to see *you* hurt, Meg. That is why I beg you to leave her service and make a different life for yourself.'

'As a housebound drudge slaving for some man?' I asked tartly. 'Ah, no, Master Villier, have no fear for me. I love my life as it is and will continue with it for as long as is possible. I love my lady, also, and all that she brings so generously into my days with her.'

'You do not love me?'

I caught my breath, then turned away from his searching eyes. Did I love Richard Villier? Yes, perhaps I did. But he was not part of my life as Penelope Rich was. I did not know him as I did my lady; did not know his family and his friends; did not see him every day in joy, and in sadness. He was away from Court for long periods, as were we, and I could not know my real feelings for him, nor envisage a life spent always in his company.

'I do not know how I feel about you,' I answered, 'save that I enjoy talking with you, and am always happy when I know you to be at Court.'

'Do you miss me when I am not?'

I shook my head. 'I cannot honestly say yes to that. This is why I must remain with my lady. When I am with her the days are always busy and filled with laughter and excitement. Except when we are at Leighs Priory,' I went on quickly. 'But even when we are there I need to be with her, for we comfort each other, and remember past joys, and look forward to when we can be at Court again. We are the best of companions, sir, and I do not believe that either of us would be totally happy without the other.'

'I think you only speak for yourself,' said Richard. 'I am sure Lady Rich would be quite capable of enjoying herself without you. She is a strong lady, Meg, and I doubt whether you possess such strength.'

'Do not worry about me.' I put out my hand and touched his sleeve. 'I have made my decision and am prepared to bear the consequences. I must leave you now and return to our chamber, but thank you for spending time with me. I am not a very comforting person to be with, am I?'

He took my outstretched hand and held it to his lips.

'Comforting, no — loving, no — sensible, no! But unfortunately you have run away with my heart, Meg Dawlish, and I can do nothing but wait, and hope that one day it will be returned to me.'

Tears pricked at my eyes and I drew my hand away from his warm clasp and hurried once more to the door. It was no good seeing him so much. He was right, and I *was* stupid! Here was a man who loved me, who would make a most good and gentle husband, of that there was no doubt. Yet I could not accept him but must return always to my Lady Penelope.

So, leave him alone, I thought fiercely, flinging open the door and hurrying away down the corridor before he should see my face. Leave Richard Villier alone, and allow him to find some other maid who will be more charitable towards him.

And how I should hate her, I cried, deep inside my selfish heart. How I would detest any female who took Richard's love away from me!

Yet why should he love me? And why should he be made to suffer from unrequited love? If he saw me no more he would soon forget Meg Dawlish and her heart of ice, and I would see my life progressing in the way I had always intended — servant to Lady Rich until death parted us.

Right, Margaret Dawlish, I decided, stand by your decision and let that man go.

Fortunately, such a plan was easy enough to achieve for Lady Penelope's life was so busy, we seemed to be always on the move, and, perhaps with intent, I saw Richard Villier no more at Court.

The year of 1588 saw further drama

in our lives, so that I knew for certain it was right to ignore Richard's advice. With Lady Penelope I experienced more in the way of intrigue and excitement than I could ever take part in as a country gentleman's wife.

First of all there was a quarrel between the Earl of Essex and Sir Charles Blount.

My poor lady was most upset by it all, because it was between the two men she loved, but I was enthralled by the news and hoped that the outcome would bring Essex down a notch, or two.

Robert Devereux had become too big for his boots during the past year, and the Queen had been showing undue attention to him, which had not helped his modesty. Then Sir Charles Blount, also young and handsome, had appeared on the scene, and Essex looked upon him as a rival.

At one of the tilting jousts held at the Palace, Blount had distinguished himself and the Queen sent him a golden chess-piece queen, richly enamelled, as a reward. He then fastened the piece on his arm with a crimson ribbon to wear as a favour.

Essex was both jealous and angry and shouted out for all to hear —

'Now I see that every fool must wear a favour!'

Lady Penelope tried to soothe both her brother, and the man she loved, but Sir Charles showed true spirit and challenged Essex to a duel. They met in Marylebone Park and Sir Charles managed to disarm my lady's brother, at the same time wounding him slightly in the thigh.

Lady Penelope comforted her brother and helped see to his wound, which was nothing to worry about at all. Essex, however, made a terrible fuss about it and needed my lady with him for several days, to talk to, explain his grievances to, and at the same time making the most of her sympathy and loving flattery.

I looked at Robert Devereux' petulant mouth and big, pansy eyes and wondered how so many females could adore him. For it was not only his mother, and his sisters, and the Queen, who loved him; many ladies at Court were equally besotted. In a way, it was easy to understand the young man's conceit, for how could he behave and think like a normal, level-headed male when so many females fawned over him? However, it was to be hoped that his defeat by Sir Charles Blount would make a humbler person of him.

After that small battle came the mighty force of the Spanish Armada against us, and the magnificent victory for England. This was followed by numerous banquets and masques at Court in celebration of our success. Against my will, I found my eyes searching for Richard Villier amongst the crowds of gallants, courtiers, knights and heroes who filled the Palace with their jubilation and laughter during those festive days. But he could not have been at Court during that time, or else I did not see him.

Towards the end of that year life took one of its downward turns beginning with the Earl of Leicester's death.

Naturally, my lady was upset, as was her mother, the Countess of Leicester, although once again I wondered at Lettice's true feelings. She seemed more worried about being thrown out of her home at Drayton Bassett, than the fact that her husband had died. I did not know all the facts of this strange matter, for we were again at Leighs Priory then, awaiting the birth of my lady's fourth child. All I do know is that my lady received a letter from her brother at Court, telling her that their mother had been forcibly ejected from Drayton Bassett.

'Just because she is now a widow and has no man to protect her, that wretched John Robinson has taken her home away from her!'

My lady's dark eyes were wet with tears, and she was crumpling her brother's letter between nervous fingers, as if she wished it was Master

Robinson's neck.

'Hush now, my lady,' I said, bending over her and rubbing her taut shoulders. 'This will do your baby no good. Try and keep calm and tell me what is being done to assist the Countess.'

'My brother says he has written to Richard Bagot, who is our neighbour at Chartley, and has asked him to get the sheriff and go with him to claim the house back for Mother.' She sniffed and wiped her wet eyes with her fingers. 'Poor Mother, all alone now and with neither Robert nor me there to aid her.'

'Your brother will do the right thing,' I said firmly, 'and Drayton Bassett will be returned to the Countess of Leicester. Remember what you told me, madam? You said that the Devereuxs are still in power, so assuredly your brother's name will be enough to sort this affair out in a trice.'

She nodded and leaned her golden head back against my arm.

'How good to have you with me, Meg,' she whispered. 'You are so sensible, and such a comfort to me always.'

I held her close, but my mouth twisted with the memory of those very words. How strange that Lady Penelope Rich and Richard Villier should feel exactly the opposite emotions about me.

Sadly, my lady's little girl, born that November, died soon after it was baptised. Maybe it was the sorrow of Leicester's death, or the worry about her mother — I know not the cause. But it took Lady Penelope some while to recover from the loss of her fourth child.

The Queen, meanwhile, had suffered also, and to my dull mind she had loved the Earl of Leicester far more than his wife had done. On hearing of his death, Her Majesty had shut herself away in her chamber for days on end, and refused to speak to anyone. It was only when the Treasurer and other members of the Council broke the door open that she was persuaded to leave the room.

Just before my lady and I left for Leighs Priory to await the birth of her poor little child, Annie told me that the Queen had placed a letter, which Leicester had sent her, into the little pearl-covered box which she kept beside her bed.

He had been on his way to take the baths at Buxton, hoping to regain his health, but this was not to be. He had died on the 4th September, having written to the Queen at one of the halts on his journey.

The Queen had the words 'His Last Letter' inscribed on it, then placed it carefully in the box underneath her rings.

7

The following year, for the first time since I had been with Lady Penelope, I wondered if perhaps Richard Villier was right in his thoughts about her, and whether I was wrong in saying that I would never leave her.

She surprised me by being unsympathetic towards me, something she had never been for as long as we had been together.

Maybe it was because she loved Sir Charles Blount, yet could not show her true feelings towards him; or maybe she was still upset by her baby's death; but for whatever reason, she lacked understanding towards me, and did not want to know how I felt at all.

Unfortunately, our disagreement involved her brother, and it should have been clear to me by then that Robert Devereux, Earl of Essex, could do no wrong in his sister's eyes.

Walter Devereux, the youngest son and last of Lettice's four children to marry, had wed Margaret Dakins, an heiress, and the families had gathered together to celebrate the union.

The Earl of Essex had been present, of course, and there had been much drinking and making merry, so much so, indeed, that I had wearied of the noisy roistering and had gone upstairs to prepare my lady's bed for her eventual retirement.

Lord Rich was not with us at that time, so I did not know at what hour to expect my lady, but waited patiently in her chamber, almost wishing that her husband was there, for then at least, my lady went to bed at a reasonable hour. And I was tired.

Suddenly, the door to the chamber was flung open and I saw Essex standing before me, a fine figure in his deep blue satin doublet, above turquoise-coloured trunk hose. A short, black velvet cloak hung from his broad shoulders, and pale blue silk encased his long legs. He reminded me of a peacock in his rich, shining garments.

'So this is where you are hiding,' he said slowly, gazing across at me with his dark Devereux eyes. Yet, unlike my lady's, for his were bloodshot and heavy from the drink he had been consuming all that day.

I rose from the stool on which I had been sitting waiting.

'Does my lady want me?' I asked.

'Nay, not my sweet Penelope, she is busily engaged in the Great Hall with the music and dancing.'

'Then who requires my service?' I was puzzled, and wished that he would say what he wanted and then remove himself from my presence.

'I want you, Meg, and will have you this night, as I have long intended.' Essex swung round to close the door behind him, then advanced on me, unfastening the brooch which held his cloak in place on his shoulder.

'You have no right to be here, sir!' I

exclaimed, backing away from him, feeling my heart beginning to pound beneath my bodice.

What an insufferable young man! And so conceited that he believed every female would be delighted to bed with him.

'I have had my eye on you ever since you first came to visit Chartley with Penelope. But what a difficult creature you are, little Meg! I admire you from afar, and when I come closer — you have vanished.'

I did not know, how could I? He was always surrounded by so many admiring females, or else occupied with the Queen in her private apartments. But if I *had* known of his interest I would have made myself even more invisible. Robert Devereux did not attract me in the slightest; indeed, I felt nothing but distaste for him and his swaggering.

'I fear that you have come to the wrong place, and to the wrong maid,' I said stiffly, standing firm before him and determined not to show fear.

The great four-poster was beside me, impossible to climb over in my long skirts, and my back was to the wall with a window on the other side of me. Essex had me trapped as neatly as a rabbit, but he would not have his way with me.

'Come, Meg, let us not play games with each other. At least, not verbal ones.' He smiled, grasping my shoulders with heavy hands and attempting to push me onto the bed.

'There are many ladies downstairs who would delight in your games, sir. So go and find one of them and leave me in peace. I am a virgin and intend remaining so. Unhand me, sir!'

I struggled to free myself from his grasp, but he held me so tightly that I could not escape his embrace.

'Never a virgin! Not in my dear sister's company,' he breathed, trying to reach my lips with his wet mouth. 'But if you are, pretty Meg, then what a joy for me, and what a reward for you. The first man in is the Earl of Essex

— Queen Elizabeth's favourite, and England's adored young man! Be proud, Meg, and take pleasure in my love.'

He had my shoulders in his grip, but my hands were free. Desperately, I clutched at my skirts and lifted them as high as I could. Then I raised my right knee and hit him between his silken thighs.

The force of the blow hurt my knee-cap but my effort had not been in vain. Letting out a yelp of pain, Essex allowed me my freedom whilst he rolled sideways onto the bed, his legs curling up towards his satin-clad chest.

I raised my skirts again and ran from the room, panting with distress at what he had tried to do, and at what I had done.

Had he power like the Queen? Could he have me sent to the Tower for assaulting his person? Could I be punished for refusing him? I did not know; had never been in such a dreadful position before; was only aware of Essex's power at Court, his prestige, and his fame. For he had taken over the role that his stepfather had played for so many years, and he was almost as important now as the great Leicester had been.

Could one refuse the Earl of Essex something he desired, and not be punished?

I made my way up two flights of stairs and hid away in an unused chamber, wondering what my lady would think about my action, and whether her brother would tell her the truth.

I also dreaded going down on the morrow and having to face the young earl's anger. Fortunately, we were due to leave next day and return to Leighs Priory, so I might not have to see Essex again for some while, and would be able to explain everything to Lady Penelope in my own words.

Strangely, Lady Penelope Rich did not see things in the same way as her servant. She obviously knew nothing of the matter when I went downstairs to see her next morning, only asking where I had been all night.

'No doubt enjoying yourself, as I was, dear Meg,' she said lightly, as we prepared to depart. 'But I should be grateful in future if you could come back somewhat sooner to my chamber, to help me disrobe. I had great difficulty in removing my attire before going to bed, and nobody seemed to know where you had disappeared to.'

I started to explain, but she put out a hand and stopped me.

'Not now, Meg. We must take our leave and return to Leighs Priory at once. Help me with my hair, and hurry. We are going to be late back as it is.'

Silently, I arranged her hair and adjusted her outer garments, determined to tell her the whole story once we had some time on our own. I wanted my lady to know exactly how I felt about her brother, and gain her assurance that I would never be placed in such an unpleasant situation again.

On our return to Leighs Priory the first days were taken up with her family, the children she adored, and who were growing so quickly now that we noticed the change in them if we were away at Court but for a couple of weeks.

Lettice, nearly seven years old, with the same golden hair and black eyes as her mother, and such a pretty child; Essex, five, and to my mind not nearly as attractive as her older sister. Maybe her name affected me unduly, but she was going to be a darker-haired maid, and possessed thicker features, looking more like her father each time I saw her.

Robert was a little darling, only two years old, but a sturdy, strong lad, and both his mother's and his father's pride and joy. He was also fair-haired, with the Devereux eyes, but it was yet too early to tell if he would retain his buttercup locks. He was extremely spoilt, being the only son, and I hoped that Lady Penelope would produce some more boys for Lord Rich.

Otherwise, it seemed to me, the child would grow up as petted and conceited as his Uncle Robert.

Once we had settled down to our severe and puritanical existence once more, and my lady had sorted out some household problems which had occurred during our absence, and I had been across to see dear Kate and the Tredworthys, I managed to speak to Lady Penelope about my experience with her brother.

'Do you mean to tell me that you ran away and hid all that night?' she asked, her black eyes opening wide and her mouth falling open in astonishment. 'Why, Meg Dawlish, what a ninny you are!'

'I do not understand you, madam,' I replied coldly. 'The earl was forcing me against my will and I was very frightened.'

'You are not only a ninny, but also a prude,' she snapped. 'Why, any other girl would jump at the opportunity to bed with my brother! Perhaps too many days spent here at Leighs have frosted you into the Rich atmosphere — affecting you both mentally and physically.'

'But I do not love the Earl of Essex.'

'I cannot think why not, for he is the most handsome, charming and adorable young man I have ever seen, at Court or elsewhere. But love matters not in such cases — we cannot always bed with the man we desire, Meg. Look at me with Lord Rich. Think you that I *enjoy* our nightly embraces? It is a woman's duty to please the man, and the fact that Essex desired *you* should have been enough. Think of his prestige, Meg, and his influence at Court. How could you be so foolish as to refuse him?'

'I hate him,' I said, and the moment those words were out I regretted them.

My lady looked at me with a face of stone; her usually full-lipped mouth was clamped shut, and her great black eyes burned with what could only be described as dislike.

But Lady Penelope could not dislike

me; we had been together for more than seven years; I had comforted her, helped her and loved her through all those days, and never once had we argued or disagreed about anything. And she had told me that I was her comfort, that she could not live without me. Could all these feelings change so rapidly because of a few careless words spoken about her brother?

'If that is how you feel I cannot change your heart, but I will warn you to have a care, Meg Dawlish, and guard your tongue. It may be that Essex will become a very powerful man indeed and, if so, it will be pleasanter to be regarded as his friend, rather than his enemy.'

Lady Penelope rose from her chair and turned her back on me to walk to the window. 'My brother and I have been in touch with King James of Scotland, who will take over the throne of England on the Queen's death. I can assure you that my brother will then rise higher than he is at present, under the somewhat bullying and waspish hands of our ageing sovereign.'

My heart sank, and I felt my stomach churn with dread at these fateful words. Always before my lady had spoken with respect for the Queen, and I had imagined that she was fond of her royal mistress. But now it looked as if there were plots afoot, political intrigues about which I knew nothing, and most certainly did not want to know.

Too many heads had rolled on the stones at Tower Hill in the past, many more could fall at the faintest whisper of treason. And to speak about the Queen's death, and announce her successor in the same breath, would most certainly amount to treason if heard by the wrong ears.

I feared for my lady then, forgetting my own distress momentarily, and wished fervently that she was not so enamoured of her brother.

Essex was conceited, hot-headed, and very ambitious; he was the Queen's favourite for most of the time, but there were several other men at Court, including Sir Charles Blount, whose names Her Majesty would use to taunt him with, whenever she wanted to annoy him.

It seemed to me as if Queen Elizabeth enjoyed having these young men about her, and encouraged them to fight and compete against each other, in order to gain her favour. One day she liked one, the next day she preferred another one. It was a difficult, tantalising atmosphere in which to live, and spoilt Robert Devereux obviously found it maddening at times.

Although I cared not one jot about Essex, I did care about my Lady Penelope, and feared that her brother's wild temperament might one day destroy them both.

Swallowing my pride, I bowed my head and asked pardon of my lady.

'Forgive me for speaking in that rude way about the Earl of Essex, madam.'

She shrugged, still annoyed by my words, and we spent the rest of that day in an unusual and strained silence.

The rest of the year passed slowly, and my lady and I continued in a formal state as mistress and maid. She no longer took me into her confidence, and twice she went away from Leighs Priory without me.

'I want to congratulate my brother on his bravery in Portugal,' she announced, as I dressed her in a beautiful gown of emerald-coloured satin, which she could only wear at Court. 'He has returned from Drake's expedition to Lisbon, and although they did not manage to free the people from their Spanish yoke, Robert displayed great courage during combat.'

Lady Penelope flashed me a taunting look from her black eyes.

'As you do not like the earl, Meg, and would find no pleasure in accompanying me to see him, I shall leave you behind.'

She swept out to the courtyard, taking enough servants with her on the journey to make sure that she would be well attended, despite my absence.

Later, when I was allowed to return to Court, I heard the whole story from Annie.

She said that Essex had deliberately ignored the Queen's demand that he should remain in England, and had gone to great lengths to join Drake's expedition. He had taken a fast hunting-horse, and covered his body in a plain, dark cloak in order to escape recognition. Then, after ninety miles of hard riding, Essex had changed to a fresh mount and reached Plymouth without being stopped.

The expedition was to prove a disappointment, however, with the English being forced to remain outside the walls of Lisbon. The only thing for which the Earl of Essex could be proud, was the fact that he had ridden alone to the city gates and driven his pike deep into the wood. Then he had dared any Spaniard within to come out and break a lance in dispute over the honour of his mistress, Queen Elizabeth.

Apparently, no man in the garrison dared — so that was the end of Robert Devereux' heroism.

He received a fierce letter from the Queen, Annie went on, with bated breath, ordering him home at once to carry out his correct duties as Master of Horse. Everyone was discussing this at Court, she said, and wondering how he had dared to defy Her Majesty.

To my ears this was all too typical of the Earl of Essex, who seemed to be always swaggering, shouting, displaying like a peacock — yet achieving little. But the people of London had taken him to their hearts and he was cheered by delighted crowds whenever he rode out, or crossed the river to go to the theatres on the opposite bank of the Thames.

'I do not understand it,' I said to Annie, when she had finished her tale, 'the people display affection for him almost as if he were of Royal blood!'

'You do not like the earl, Meg, and

therefore nothing he does will ever find admiration in your eyes,' she answered. 'But *I* think he is the handsomest young man I have ever seen, and the people adore him because he is such a romantic figure. Think of it. Essex is but twenty-two years old, and he has stood up to the Queen, duelled with Sir Charles Blount; he hates Sir Walter Raleigh and has the courage to say so; he has equal courage in outwitting Her Majesty and escaping on a sea voyage; and he thrusts his lance into the gates of Lisbon and challenges the hated Spanish to a fight. Of *course* he is a hero, in most people's eyes, and with both Sir Philip Sidney, and the Earl of Leicester gone, he is the only young knight we have left to adore.'

I blinked at her words, then nodded, not wanting to arouse her anger as I had earlier aroused my lady's. I could not feel the same love and admiration shared by so many for Robert Devereux, but I could accept their views, and had just to be careful never to speak my mind whilst in their company.

The second time that Lady Penelope left me behind at Leighs Priory was when she attended her mother's marriage. Lettice was wed for the third time to Sir Christopher Blount, a man many years younger than she was. He was a kinsman of Sir Charles Blount, and had been the Earl of Leicester's Master of Horse.

This proved to me yet again that my lady's mother was a selfish creature. How could she marry again so soon after her last husband's death?

After my lady returned from that celebration, she appeared in a gentler frame of mind, and later I was to realise that she and Sir Charles had come to an agreement at that time, which delighted her and made her a happier person.

It was fortunate for me that Lady Penelope did treat me with more kindness, for my dearest Kate Haddock died that summer, and with both my mistress leaving me alone so much, and the loss of my other dear companion and friend, I felt very bereft. Luckily for me I could still visit the Tredworthys, and Mary was a great solace at that time; speaking little, but listening to me whenever I wanted to unburden my heart, and comforting me with her gentleness every time I called at the crowded rooms above the stables.

Once my Lady Penelope had found her own personal contentment, however, she needed me beside her, as before, and I did not often find time to revisit Kate's family.

One evening, my lady put her arm around me and said,

'Ah, Meg, I have missed your sensible and loving company. Let us be friends again, for there is much excitement afoot and one day, my Meg, we will have a new home to enjoy, and pleasanter company than that found in this miserable household.'

This new home and pleasanter company took some while to enter our lives, for once again Lady Penelope was with child, and, being the person she was, she could not start her life with a new man until she had completed her time with the old.

The only thing which surprised me, and never ceased to cause me some astonishment, was the fact that Lord Rich allowed my lady to continue along the path which she and Sir Charles Blount had laid out for themselves the year before.

Although my lady was not to share her husband's bed again after the spring of 1590, the babies she produced after that date were all known as Rich, and she continued to go to Leighs Priory when her husband called for her. Sometimes it was because he was ill and needed her attention, and some-times because he required her clever brain to help him on a legal matter, or a difficult letter which needed to be written carefully. I could only assume, as Lady Penelope had once told me, that Lord Rich found it useful having a brother-in-law at Court, and a favourite of Her Majesty, at that; and he feared to divorce his wife, knowing that in so doing he would arouse the Earl of Essex's anger and enmity.

Of course, the arrangement suited my lady very well, for each time she went back to Leighs Priory, she saw her children, and as she produced more for Sir Charles, the country home in Essex made a perfect and happy place in which to grow up.

I found it hard, however, to understand how a bully like Lord Rich could be so weak in other matters. He *knew* of his wife's love-affair with Sir Charles, he *knew* that the babies which appeared after that year were not his; his wife no longer shared his bed, and yet she continued to bear his name. He knew all these unpleasant facts, and he said nothing.

I could feel no sympathy for the man, only scorn, and was never able to condemn my lady for her future behaviour as mistress of Sir Charles

Blount. With him she was truly happy, totally content, and they were ideally suited although, perhaps, Sir Charles liked the countryside better than Lady Penelope. The saddest part was that they had not met earlier, whilst my lady was still a maid, and thus been allowed to marry and live their lives properly as husband and wife.

Lady Penelope's second son was born in August, and named Henry. At least she had done her duty by Lord Rich and produced two healthy sons for him, as well as the two little girls, so he should have been well satisfied. Once she had regained her strength, she set off to meet the man she loved, and our new life began.

Unfortunately for me, it proved to be at Essex House in the Strand, the home of her brother. But once I had been shown my lady's apartment, and realised in what great and lavish style the Earl of Essex entertained, with one hundred and sixty servants, I hoped that there would be little chance of him noticing me.

Lady Penelope's chamber was truly magnificent and far more beautiful than the one she had at Leighs Priory. The bed was in black, gold and silver, with a black canopy trimmed with gold and black damask, and black curtains edged with gold lace. The chairs and stools were of black velvet with gilt frames, and the cushions were of cloth of silver. It was a room made for lovers, and I understood my lady's happiness; it was the last possible kind of chamber in which to envisage Lord Rich.

'Sir Charles will not actually live here,' said my lady, her eyes sparkling as black and shiny as the satin of her gown.

Everyone was wearing black and white at Court these days, they were said to be the Queen's favourite colours, but I preferred Lady Penelope in the brighter reds, and blues, and greens which she normally favoured. 'He has his own house in Holborn and it would not be right for him to take up residence here, but he will visit as often as he likes. Charles and Robert have become good friends since that foolish quarrel, and my brother has said that Charles may come here whenever he and I are away from Court.'

'And the Queen?' I queried, knowing what Her Majesty was like with the behaviour of her courtiers and their female companions.

Some months earlier the Earl of Essex had married Frances, the widow of Sir Philip Sidney. This marriage had been concealed from the Queen for some time, but eventually she found out, and was furious. As was typical of her, her anger was against Frances rather than Essex, so Frances was banished from Court life whilst her husband carried on in normal fashion.

My lady told me that Frances, now Lady Essex, was not unduly worried by her exclusion from Court as she was a quiet, retiring sort of person. So she now lived with her mother, who was newly widowed, at their home in

160

Walsingham House in Seething Lane, or at Barn Elms, in Putney.

'Both houses are on the Thames,' my lady had informed me, 'and Robert can take the boat from Essex Stairs and visit her whenever he wishes.'

Now, I wondered how the Queen would react when she knew of the relationship between Lady Penelope Rich and Sir Charles Blount.

'We are hopeful that Her Majesty will not find out,' answered my lady, running her slender fingers over the velvet-covered chair beside her. 'Charles and I mean to be discreet about our love for each other, and as I cannot abide secrets, or the telling of lies, we will stay here openly and allow our best friends to know the truth. As Robert entertains hugely, and is forever providing great banquets and theatrical entertainments here, there are so many guests that I do not believe our presence together will be unduly noticed.'

'I hope it will not cause you trouble, my lady. It would be most upsetting if you were to be banished, like your mother and your new sister-in-law. You would never be content away from Court life.'

She shook her head. 'Heaven forbid!' she exclaimed. 'But then you would not like that either, would you, my Meg? You enjoy visiting Court just as much as I do.'

I smiled in agreement. My lady had spoilt me in that respect, and I knew that she was right and no life in the countryside would ever compare favourably with that of Court.

'Then be careful,' I said, 'for neither of us want these days to end.'

'I shall leave it all to Charles and do whatever he advises. He is most sensible, Meg, rather like you, and will always know what is best to do. Fortunately, the Queen is very pleased with him and likes to have him near her. She admires his studious mind, and his quiet, gentle manners. Charles is somewhat different to her other favourites, being as happy when reading a book as he is when riding into battle. Oh, I am a lucky woman, Meg, and still cannot believe that Charles really loves me.'

She twirled about the room in her black satin gown, with the underdress of orange silk, the Devereux colour, which also helped to alleviate the blackness of her gown. Then she raised both arms above her head in an ecstasy of joy.

'Will you remain here at Essex House all the time?' I asked, watching her graceful movements. How happy she was now, and how different to the sedate, controlled behaviour she had to maintain all the time when we were at Leighs Priory.

'I shall have to go back to my husband when he requires it,' she said slowly, folding her mouth into a prim grimace and pausing in her dance. 'But we will be husband and wife in name only from now on, Meg. I have made that quite clear to him. Unfortunately, I am still Lady Rich, so must go when he calls, but I shall not go gladly, nor swiftly, and we will stay at Leighs for very short periods, be assured of that!'

I saw Sir Charles Blount properly for the first time that evening, and knew at once that he was the perfect partner for my lady. He was tall and handsome, most neat in appearance and in all movement, and so gentle with Lady Penelope that I rejoiced in the fact that she had found such a caring and affectionate man.

Those were splendid days indeed, with my lady in love and so animated and beautiful that she had many admirers. To my relief she managed her life exceedingly well, and was accepted at Court as readily as before.

On the 17th November, 1590, at the tournament to celebrate the Queen's Accession Day, Sir Charles rode to the tilts wearing my lady's colours of orange and white, as his courtly favours. No royal outburst followed, and it seemed to me that Sir Charles and Lady Penelope had arranged a perfect life for themselves.

8

Essex House was continually crowded with people, and my lady was forever telling me about the interesting folk who congregated there. The Earl of Southampton was one, I remember, who was a very great friend of Robert Devereux, and on several occasions he brought a young man with him named Will Shakespeare. Will was a dramatist who had come to London a few years before, and had begun to make his name with the writing of plays.

The Earls of Southampton and Essex were patrons of literature, and my lady became most interested herself, so that many different authors dedicated their works to her.

'Astrophil and Stella' was first published in 1591, and my lady was overjoyed to see Sir Philip Sidney's great words at last in print, but it was not yet obvious to all that Lady Penelope was 'Stella', because the three sonnets which used the name Rich so cleverly were not in the first two editions. This made no difference to her closest friends, for they knew the truth already. As it was, many new young writers were busily scribbling their sonnets, hoping to achieve Sir Philip Sidney's fame, and my lady's name was often used by them.

It did not surprise me at the time, but looking back I am amazed at the extent in which we travelled during those years of the 1590s.

My lady appeared at Court often, and spent many contented hours with her lover, and numerous friends, at Essex House. But we also visited her mother in Staffordshire, her brother's home at Chartley, and, of course, Lord Rich in Essex, when he demanded a visit from his wife. My lady did not enjoy seeing him again, but she did love playing with her children, and it was always difficult for her to wrench herself away from them.

We visited her sister-in-law, Frances, in the January of 1591 as she was expecting her first baby by Essex, and my lady insisted on remaining with her until the child arrived. It was a little girl, named Penelope after my lady.

I know my lady missed her own children and after seeing her sister-in-law's darling babe she was very quiet, and I wondered if she would dare to produce a bastard child by Sir Charles.

Of course Lady Penelope dared — she never lacked for courage, and the following year another little Penelope was born, and baptised on the 30th March at St Clement Danes church just opposite Essex House in the Strand.

That year, too, the plague swept through London and all the theatres closed. As the Queen ventured forth on one of her annual Progresses, my lady decided that she, too, would enjoy the freshness of some country air for a while, so off we went to Staffordshire.

Whilst we were staying at Chartley, I

saw Richard Villier again. My heart gave an unexpected lurch of joy as I saw his tall figure advancing towards me, making me realise how much I had missed him. He looked most handsome in his green velvet doublet, which exactly matched the colour of his eyes, and bowed low over my hand as if I were a high-born lady.

'I have missed you, Meg Dawlish,' he said, straightening his body and gazing down at me with admiration. 'Dare I ask if you have missed me?'

I smiled up at him, feeling my cheeks beginning to glow.

'I cannot say that I have thought about you every day,' I answered demurely, 'but must admit that it is very pleasant to see you again, Master Villier.'

'With those terse words I must be satisfied, I suppose. But tell me, Meg, has your heart not begun to thaw beneath that deep red bodice of yours?'

I was wearing one of Lady Penelope's cast-off brocades, with sleeves slashed with white silk. I knew that the dark red suited me probably better than my lady, because of my dark hair, and felt myself to be almost beautiful. Knowing that Richard Villier could see me so attired made me feel even more content.

'I have a heart, sir,' I answered him, 'but it is settled entirely upon Lady Penelope at present. And so many interesting things have been happening to us, I cannot sit around all day wondering what a certain gentleman is doing with his time.'

'Indeed not, and there are such charming and courageous men at Court, I feel sure they must be of greater interest to you. I hear that Lady Rich is seen much at Essex House these days. No doubt you accompany her there, and are enthralled by her brother's charm and good looks?'

'I do not admire the Earl of Essex,' I replied stiffly, turning my face away from Richard's penetrating gaze. 'But fortunately, he has not spoken to me at his great house in the Strand.'

'That is strange, for he has an eye for beautiful women, and you are growing lovelier every time I see you, Meg.'

Again the blood rushed to my cheeks, and I endeavoured to hide my emotions by fluttering the little fan before my face, which Lady Penelope had given me as a New Year's gift.

How would it have been if Richard Villier had surprised me in my lady's bedchamber that night of the wedding? Would I have felt dislike and fear at his unexpected visit? Or would I have fallen into his arms as readily as any lovesick maid? It was disconcerting to admit secretly, deep within my heart, that I would probably have given in, and gladly.

'Do not tell me that Robert Devereux' attentions have been refused? I can scarce believe that!' Richard's voice was mocking, and his eyes fairly snapped with glee. 'Why, every maid at Court is madly in love with the Queen's favourite, and he can take his pick from any of the attendants when he is not with Her Majesty. Or so I have been informed.'

'I do not have anything to do with Her Majesty, for I am but a servant,' I answered briskly, thankful to take seductive thoughts of my companion off my mind. 'Do not tease, I beg. The first argument I ever had with my lady concerned her brother, and I hope never to arouse her wrath again.'

'So? Life is not so rosy with the fair Penelope Rich? I am delighted to hear that. But for the sake of Heaven beware of young Essex, Meg. He is a hot-tempered, spoilt lad and will have his way, no matter what. How the Queen puts up with him, I do not know, save that she is growing old now and, I think, has never got over Leicester's death.'

'I am fully aware of the earl's behaviour, and will avoid him like the plague. Do not worry about me, sir, for I have a good head on my shoulders and can look after myself.'

'I think not.' Richard put out his

hand and took hold of mine, raising it against his chest. 'Let me look after you, Meg. If you have had one argument with Lady Rich who knows when there will be another? And she will never take your side against her brother. She is totally enamoured of him, as are all the Devereux women.'

'I know.' I tried to remove my hand from his warm grasp without success. 'But Essex is now happily married, I have not seen him except at a distance for more than a year, and Sir Charles Blount is a good man and would take my part, I know, if anything unpleasant should occur.'

'Blount is a good man, I agree, but he is in love, Meg, and Lady Penelope could make him do whatever she desired. Do not believe that he would champion you against Essex, or I fear that you will be sadly disillusioned one day.'

* * *

In July of that year, there was excitement for my lady, and all at Essex House, when the Earl was given permission by the Queen to take a force across the Channel to assist the French against the Spanish, who had recently invaded north-western France.

There was a parade of soldiers before the Queen, and Lady Penelope took me along with her to see the splendidly-attired force — which her brother was taking with him to France.

'Robert has spent fourteen thousand pounds equipping and dressing his men,' my lady told me, 'and they are magnificent in their orange and white liveries, are they not, Meg? See how proudly they wear the Devereux colours.'

I looked and saw, and agreed that they were very fine but wondered, silently, how a young man who was heavily in debt could afford such a huge sum of money.

In August, we heard that the Earl of Essex had landed with his army at

Dieppe, and my lady informed me that her younger brother, Walter, had also joined the orange and white army, making it a very special Devereux affair.

Messengers were continually travelling to and from Court, keeping the Queen in touch with what was going on abroad, and thus my lady, also, heard what was happening to her beloved Robert.

'He has met King Henri at Compiègne, and apparently his entry was quite magnificent. Oh, Meg, how proud I am of my dearest Robin!'

She went on to say that six pages rode before Essex dressed in their orange velvet, embroidered with gold, and the Earl, himself, wore a military cloak of orange velvet, covered with jewels. His saddle, bridle, and horse's harness were all fashioned in the same colours, and six trumpeters sounded his entry into Compiègne.

Then the news was not so good, for we heard that whilst the English army was camped outside Dieppe, malaria and dysentery swept through the ranks and Essex, also, succumbed to the fever. To make matters considerably worse for my lady, we heard that Walter Devereux, the young man whom we had seen married but two short years before, had been killed outside the walls of Rouen. He was struck through the cheek by a bullet, which pierced up through his skull.

My lady wept when she told me, and it was reported that Robert Devereux also wept, lying in his tent and laid low with both the fever, and the tragic personal loss.

The Queen, however, showed little pity for her earl, and had him back at Court once he was fit enough to travel. Apparently, he had not behaved to her liking and after a very short stay in the Royal Presence, Essex was sent back to Dieppe with instructions to behave like a general.

All this to-ing and fro-ing was quite beyond my simple brain, and as my lady stormed between Court and Essex

House with tight lips, showing none of her usual gaiety, I decided not to ask her any awkward questions. Not for the first time in my life I was thankful to be a mere nobody; without prestige, power, or Royal patronage.

I had never felt affection for the Queen, and wondered sometimes why Essex should spend so much of his time, and his wealth, and his emotions, on his Royal Mistress. Presumably, he did so for the rewards which such companionship and acclaim could bring him, and he was young, and very ambitious. But nonetheless, good times were followed by bad, and I hoped that the wild and reckless young Devereux, whom so many people adored, would possess the strength and cool self-discipline needed, if ever faced with Her Majesty's cruel wrath.

In November, Rouen was finally besieged; the Queen was pleased with Essex and ordered him home. Yet, once back at Court, news came that Spanish troops were on the move from the

Netherlands towards Rouen, so Essex was sent back to France.

This time he remained until January of the following year, before handing over command to Sir Roger Williams.

'And about time too!' said Lady Penelope indignantly. 'Poor Robin has spent far too much of his precious time in that miserable country. He has written that sickness is spreading so rapidly through his troops, that he will be fortunate in bringing *any* home alive. Now Sir Roger can go over and do his fair share of command and Robin can come home for good.'

That winter Richard Villier's fears were proved correct, and I was made to realise that my future with Lady Penelope was not as golden as I had supposed.

As the theatres were closed because of plague, Robert Devereux arranged many theatrical performances at Essex House, to celebrate his return from France, and after one such entertainment he tricked me into entering his part of the house.

Normally, I helped my lady to retire for bed, and then made myself scarce in a small niche adjoining her chamber. There I had my truckle-bed and as the chamber was very large and the huge four-poster bed, shared by my lady and Sir Charles, was heavily curtained, I was not disturbed by them, nor were they aware of me.

But this night, before the guests had retired, a man-servant came to me and told me that Lady Penelope required my presence. I followed him, unaware that he was leading me into danger.

Essex House was so vast, there were so many passages and adjoining rooms, that I followed the man blindly until he led me into the presence of the Earl of Essex.

There were several servants with him, but he waved them away when I appeared and told them to watch the door.

'I am not to be disturbed until I give word,' he called out, placing his hands upon my shoulders and stopping my flight as everyone else left the chamber.

'So, Meg Dawlish, we meet again.' His brown eyes were alight with lust, and his full lips shone wet in the candle-light. 'You escaped me last time,' he said softly, 'but I learned my lesson then and will not allow the same thing to happen now.'

He had grown a beard whilst he had been away, and the hair on his face was as strong a red-brown as the thick hair on his head. Robert Devereux was also broader-shouldered, and seemed taller than when I had last seen him. Before, he had been a slim, arrogant youth but his command of the forces abroad had turned Essex into a man. Despite the change in him, I could still only feel repulsion and fear for Lady Penelope's brother but this time, I knew that I was doomed. There was no one who would come to my rescue should I cry out, and the door was firmly guarded behind me.

Then let it be, I thought, closing my

eyes and holding my body stiff as a ramrod as Essex began to remove my clothing, piece by piece. But it will happen without my consent, and with hatred in my heart.

Robert Devereux was a skilled lover, I could tell that although without experience myself. His hands were warm and gentle, his mouth soft, and his words were admiring as he explored every part of my rigid body. He tried to make me find enjoyment and pleasure, that must be admitted, but I was so angry and disgusted by his knavish trick and unwanted attention, that I could not respond to his caresses.

At last, with an exclamation of annoyance, Devereux gave up trying to entice me, and entered my unwilling body with the strength and sharpness of a sword.

I cried out then, in pain and revolt, but he twined my loosened hair between his fingers and continued thrusting — deep within me as if he would never stop. Finally it was over, and he rolled away from me, satiated and exhausted.

Very slowly I moved my aching limbs away from his sleeping form and endeavoured to sit up. I was bruised and bleeding, both inside and out, and stupid, useless tears began to stream down my face. I dressed as best I could and found a few scattered pins to hold up my hair, then walked painfully to the door.

Several men lounged on the floor outside, and a young page drowsed, propping himself against the doorpost. After one look at my face, the two who were awake allowed me to pass, with a burst of laughter and several coarse jests at my retreating back.

It took me a long time to drag myself back to the rooms belonging to my lady, and on entering the main chamber I saw that she and Sir Charles had returned. Clothing was scattered about the floor and the bed curtains had been drawn together.

I wanted to wash myself clean, to

remove every trace of filth and blood from my person, but I was too tired, and there was no water left in the bowl. So I lay till morning, wounded and dirty and unable to sleep, with my brain twisting and churning as savagely as a terrier attacking a rat.

What was to be done now? I had no money, for my lady gave me everything I wanted; shelter, food and clothing.

I had no living relative, and no friend outside the gilded life of Court circles, and the Devereux family.

I had no home to call my own, and no independence.

Everything I had, and enjoyed, and needed, was provided for by my mistress. Even the man who had so misused me, and from whom there was no escape, even he, was my Lady Penelope's brother. And the thought of having to go to Essex every time he called, made me want to vomit. Lady Penelope had had to obey Lord Rich's demands, but then he was her husband. I was not married to the Earl of Essex, yet there appeared to be no way in which I could avoid his bed.

Richard Villier had warned me of this; he was a good man and with him I could have been happily wed by now, and safe. But I had ignored his warnings, rejected his love, believing that his way of life was too dull when compared with my lady's butterfly existence.

Now it was too late. I could never bring myself to beg for Richard Villier's love, or understanding. I had brought this upon myself and must accept the consequences. But there must be a way out somehow; somewhere I would find refuge and security. I just needed time in which to think, and an idea would come.

Finally, I slept.

I did not tell Lady Penelope of my dilemma. She was so much in love with Sir Charles, and so busily engaged with her life at Court, and at Essex House, that she and I had lost our once close relationship. She still needed my care and attention, of course, but it was superficial now and our conversations were about what she would wear on each coming engagement, and how I should arrange her hair, and which jewels looked best with each new attire.

Because she was so happy with Sir Charles, she did not need my comfort and friendship any more, and I became solely her maid, to obey her wishes and give my advice on certain garments, when asked for it.

Sir Charles Blount, oddly enough, must have noticed my appearance for he stopped by me one morning, before departing from Essex House, and asked if I was feeling ill.

I almost wept as I looked up into his kind face and saw concern in his dark eyes.

'I am quite well, sir,' I answered quietly, not wanting the subject to be brought to my lady's attention. 'A touch of the migraine, that is all.'

He nodded and patted my shoulder before moving away down the corridor.

A good and caring man, I thought again, and how fortunate for Lady Penelope to be loved by such a person.

I did tell Annie about my misfortune one day, when I had accompanied my lady to Court, but received no sympathy from her.

'You are so lucky, Meg!' she cried out, when I had told her a little about that dreadful night. 'I cannot imagine why you are upset about it. Heavens, most of us would give our eyes to be seduced by Essex! Do you not realise how powerful he is becoming? And how very handsome?'

'Yes,' I answered stonily, 'I know his strength, but do not find him in any way attractive.'

'Then you are a fool! Robert Devereux is the handsomest man at Court, and the most admired and sought after man in the kingdom. Be grateful, Meg, and show him that he pleases you. Why, he might give you presents, and beautiful jewels, if you will but give in to him gracefully. Silly goose, you have the most wonderful opportunity before you. Grasp it with both hands, I would say, for it will not last long and you should gain as much as you can, whilst you can.'

Annie stared at me with envy in her eyes.

'We are not getting any younger, Meg, and must provide a bit for our futures. Do you imagine that you can continue to attend Lady Rich in your dotage? From what I have seen and heard, we are not wanted once our movements become slow and our eyesight weakens. Our mistresses may age, but they then need younger, more agile servants to care for their needs.'

I was twenty-five then, with many more years ahead of me, but what Annie was saying made me think; it was similar to the words Richard Villier had spoken, and I had ignored his advice, to my own detriment. It was depressing to have to think about the future when one should be enjoying the present; yet now that Lady Penelope no longer needed me so much my days were less interesting, and thoughts of the years ahead came more readily to mind.

There was also the continual fear of Essex.

It seemed more than likely that he would continue to demand my presence in his bedchamber, at least for the time being, and what would happen if I should bear a child by him? Would Robert Devereux provide me with money for its keep? Would he even accept that the child was his?

I had heard tales of girls with illegitimate babies, whose fathers refused to accept responsibility for their bastard offspring. Sometimes the girls had killed their babies, and once or twice I had heard of a girl who had killed herself, unable to cope with the shame and responsibility on her own.

Strangely, my solution came through the Devereux family, to whom I seemed to be bound whether I like it or not. But the help came neither from my lady, nor from her brother. It came from Dorothy, sister to Lady Penelope, who was wed to Sir Thomas Perrot.

We were at Leighs Priory for Lord Rich had sent for my lady, and she had to visit him, though against her will. In order to make her days at Leighs more agreeable, however, she had invited her mother, and her sister, and Lady Essex, her sister-in-law, to accompany her.

One morning, whilst the other ladies were out riding, Lady Dorothy called to me as I was passing down the passage on my way to the linen-room.

'I have not seen you for a long time, Meg. Come and sit with me this afternoon and let us talk a while.'

I had always been fond of my lady's sister, but since her strange marriage and banishment from Court, we had not seen so much of her. Although Lady Dorothy had produced several babies for Sir Thomas, there was only one remaining alive and the little girl was named Penelope, after her aunt.

I went to Lady Dorothy's chamber later that day, as bidden, and found her busy with some tapestry, and watching fondly as her daughter played close by.

'How is life treating you, Meg Dawlish? And are you still as happy with my sister as you were the last time we met?'

She had the same golden hair and black Devereux eyes as the rest of her family, but her face was broader than my lady's, and I found a kindness there and an interest in me — which had been missing for some time from Lady Penelope.

No doubt it was due to my worry and depression, and to the demands made on me by the Earl of Essex, that I felt the words pour out of me. But it was also due to Lady Dorothy's look of compassion.

I knew that she loved her brother, so was careful not to speak too angrily about him, but I did say that I could not love him, that I hated having to go to his bedchamber whenever he called for me, and that I desired some kind of independence above all else.

'As you are so kind as to listen to me, madam, I would dearly like your advice,' I went on, knowing exactly what I wanted.

'Go on, Meg, tell me what you have in mind.'

'I was born in London, madam, and my father was a merchant of cloth, owning a shop in Cheapside.' I told her about Mistress Gwendoline, and my flight to Essex with Kate Haddock. 'I have no knowledge of his will, but would dearly like to know if I should have inherited something as I was his only daughter. Can you tell me the best thing to do?'

Lady Dorothy smiled and laid her hands down upon her lap.

'Dear me, Meg, do I know what to do? I seem to have spent the best part of my married life writing letters for help and assistance. Firstly, there were letters to the Lord Treasurer about my poor Tom's imprisonment in the Fleet; then his father, Sir John Perrot, was most unfriendly towards us and would not send money due to us. Then I had to fight for my dowry money, left for me in my father's will, but not released because I had wed without due consent.'

I stared at her sweet face with hope in my heart. No wonder Lady Dorothy was so kind and caring — she had suffered, too.

'Should I write to the Lord Treasurer?' I asked, 'Would he know about my father's will?'

'Leave it all to me for the present, dear Meg. You will need a good lawyer and no doubt he will have to battle for your interest in the Probate Court. You will also have to prove that you are the true daughter of Master Dawlish. Give me all the facts you can; the date of your father's death, the address in Cheapside, and date of your birth. Then I will do what I can and let you know.'

I flung myself at her feet and kissed one of her white, long-fingered hands, so like her sister's in shape and colour.

'Oh, my lady, I am so grateful to you

and do not know how to thank you properly.'

'Meg, stand up and be proud,' she said sharply. 'You are a well-educated, well-born female and must always remember that. You are only a servant at present but these things can change. Go on — get up!'

Lady Dorothy gave me a little push and I arose unsteadily, wiping my wet face with my hands.

'Have faith in yourself, dear girl, and remember a father who loved you. He would never have allowed you to go forth in life without a penny to your name. It is a pity that Kate Haddock no longer lives, for she would have made a perfect witness. However, I shall endeavour to find out the truth of this matter, and see if Mistress Gwendoline can be made to part with much of what is rightfully yours.'

Confidence returned to me for the first time in many months, and I began to feel hope about my future. Lady Dorothy Perrot was the answer to my problems and with her help and experience my life must surely improve.

'Say nothing to Penelope as yet,' remarked my companion, going back to her tapestry. 'I love her dearly but she is much occupied at present with her beloved Sir Charles, and the less than loving Lord Rich. Stay quietly with her and bide your time, Meg. I promise that I will contact you once your problem has been placed into suitable hands.'

9

I heard nothing more from Lady Dorothy for some time and so had to suppress worries about my future and continue with life as it was. Fortunately for me, the Earl of Essex became more and more involved with Court life after his return from France, and spent much time with the Bacon brothers, Francis and Anthony, who became frequent visitors to Essex House.

Everyone appeared delighted when Sir Walter Raleigh was imprisoned in the Tower, as punishment for marrying one of the Queen's attendants.

'The way will be clear for Robert to climb even higher in favour,' my lady told me with glee, 'now that rogue has been put behind bars.'

'What of his wife?' I asked, thinking it very hard for a female to be newly wed and then to find her husband taken away from her and flung into prison.

But Lady Dorothy had borne such callous treatment, I reminded myself, when she had the audacity to elope with Tom Perrot without royal knowledge, or consent. And she had managed to get her husband out of Fleet Prison eventually.

My lady laughed. 'Bess Throgmorton has been put in the Tower, also, and in a separate cell from her husband. Now the only people dear Robin must worry about are the Cecils. Lord Burghley is greatly admired by the Queen, of course, but he is getting old and it is said that he is grooming his son, Robert, to take his place. Well, I think that our Robert is of far better wit, and intelligence, and charm than little hunchbacked Robert Cecil. And I cannot believe that Her Majesty will ever put her faith in a cripple.'

Once again, I was glad not to be involved in the political scene or, in fact, in any matter of importance at Court. But I kept my eyes and ears open, and was more often in my lady's confidence these days, which made life more interesting. Thus I was aware of much that went on in Essex House during the busy year of 1593 and, more important than anything else, such activity kept the Earl of Essex away from me, allowing me to relax and feel less worried about my future.

Francis and Anthony Bacon called often, sometimes living for short periods at Essex House; there was the handsome young Earl of Southampton, with the piercing eyes, who would bring his friend Will Shakespeare on social visits, and many evenings were spent, so my lady told me, in writing poetry and sonnets together. Sir Charles Danvers was there, and Henry Cuffe, who travelled much to the continent gaining information for Essex, and who was later to become his secretary.

Lady Penelope and her brother also spent much time at Court, and Robert Devereux was in the highest favour with the Queen. At the Court celebrations on Twelfth Night, Essex was Her Majesty's attendant, and danced so long and frequently with the Queen, that they appeared like lovers, my lady informed me.

'Robert was so tall and handsome beside her, I could not help myself from swelling with pride, and the Queen, albeit at a distance, looked like a young girl, Meg! And she was giggling and flirting with Robert for everyone to see.'

Lady Penelope was jubilant at the excitement of her news, but I felt strangely ill at ease. The Queen of England must now be sixty years old — how *could* she behave in such a way with a man less than half her years in age? And how could Essex appear to enjoy and be flattered by such attentions from an old lady? Knowing him as I did, with his physical abilities and delight in sexual matters, I could not understand what attracted him to the Queen, nor how he could spend so much time with her when there were plenty of young and lovely ladies who desired him.

It was almost a relief to me when we travelled to Leighs Priory that spring. For a time, at least, I would be well away from the Earl of Essex and tales of his magnificence at Court.

My lady was again with child and so we settled down to await the baby's birth. It was, of course, the second by Sir Charles Blount, and my lady now had her own bedchamber well away from Lord Rich.

The first excitement, I remember, was when Mistress Wiseman came to Leighs and told my lady all that was happening at Broadoaks. She was a neighbour of the Richs, although I had not seen her before, and her son, William, was a secret Catholic.

This afternoon, my lady allowed me to remain in the room whilst she and Mistress Wiseman chatted, and my ears fairly crackled listening to the talk.

Mistress Wiseman was a large, elderly lady, heavily attired in plum-coloured velvet. Her grey hair was covered with a lace cap and her florid face bulged over the top of her ruff.

'William has always made Broadoaks a safe place for shelter, as you must have guessed, Lady Rich,' said she, 'and last week we took in Father John Gerard, a most excellent Jesuit priest.'

Lady Penelope looked at her visitor's popping eyes and flushed cheeks. 'Go on, Mistress Wiseman, tell me more. I can see by your face that it has been an eventful few days for you. Was the priest pursued to Broadoaks?'

'Indeed he was, Lady Rich. Father Gerard has made so many converts to the faith that he is a wanted man. Well now,' she sucked in her breath and folded her fat hands tightly together. 'A wretched spy in the household informed on him, but we just managed to get him into hiding before his pursuers arrived. I will not tell you where the hiding-place is, Lady Rich, for it is better if you do not know.'

'I understand,' my lady smiled, 'and

as I do not care for pain, it would be too easy to divulge everything if put to torture, dear Mistress Wiseman.'

The elderly lady nodded sagely. 'Would you believe that the search-party remained with us for *four* days, Lady Rich, and they even lit a fire above the dear man's head, but could not find him! He existed all that time in a minute space, and ate nothing but a few biscuits and a little quince jelly.'

Lady Penelope shook her golden head in wonder. 'Is he still with you? I would like to meet your courageous priest.'

Mistress Wiseman nodded, then slanted her eyes at me. 'Can she be trusted?' she whispered.

'Of course, else she would not be present. Meg is my greatest friend and confidant. We would both like to meet this amazing man, would we not, Meg?'

I nodded in reply, but my heart had begun to thump in trepidation. My lady always enjoyed intrigue and a sense of danger, but this plan was exceedingly dangerous; for she was the wife of a well-known Puritan, and the priest was a wanted man and known to be hiding somewhere in the county of Essex.

However, my lady always did exactly what she wanted, and no doubt it amused her to bring a Catholic into such a staunch Puritan household.

'See if it can be arranged, dear Mistress Wiseman, and if your Father Gerard can spare the time, tell him that Lady Rich would be most interested in talking with him about the Catholic faith. Who knows? He might yet achieve another convert!'

My heart thumped harder at her words and I felt sick. Lady Penelope was an important person, sister to the powerful Earl of Essex, but there were some things which were forbidden no matter who you were, and being a Catholic was one of them. The Queen would never allow this to happen to a lady with such close connections at Court, and I knew that she would find out eventually, for Her Majesty had spies everywhere. Visions of the block at Tower Hill arose before my eyes, and I wished that my lady would not get so carried away with her audacious plans.

'My husband will be away from home two nights from today,' I heard Lady Penelope go on blithely, 'so that would be an ideal time for Father Gerard to come here.'

Mistress Wiseman dutifully departed with the message and two evenings later, the Jesuit priest arrived at Leighs Priory, quite openly, and spent three hours conversing with my lady.

It was all too much for me and I had a terrible migraine thinking about the possible consequences. But my lady was glowing again, thrilled by the dangerous yet tempting situation. She wrote off at once to Sir Charles, telling him of her intention to convert to Catholicism, and poor Sir Charles rushed to us from Court, in a fair pickle.

I was extremely glad to see him, for though Lady Penelope would never take notice of what I had to say, she was always most obedient with Sir Charles Blount.

Once again Lord Rich was away from home, and Sir Charles and the priest spent a long time, with Lady Penelope, behind closed doors. I was not present at any conversation with Father Gerard, and for that I was grateful. I remembered how dear Kate Haddock had warned against the Spanish, and their faith, and had heard for myself the terrible slaughter of Protestants in the Netherlands, and in France. I, certainly, wanted nothing to do with a belief which brought out such cruelty in people.

Later, I was to hear from my lady what had transpired during that secret meeting.

'Charles is so clever,' she told me, admiringly, 'and knew just what to say, and what questions to ask Father Gerard; things I would never have thought of myself, Meg. As it happened, they could agree on very little and I realised then that Charles was right, and I did not wish to be converted after all. I still *admire* the priest, Meg, and think much of his good faith. But I do not believe in everything he said, so Charles found it quite easy to dissuade me.'

I breathed a sigh of enormous relief. 'Thank heavens for that! You had me very worried for a while.'

'Dear Meg,' she placed an arm around my shoulders and gave me a hug, 'do not *worry* so. It was merely a small entertainment in this very dreary life we have here in the country. I felt like a challenge to get the blood moving once again in my stagnant veins, and that is exactly what happened.'

Thank God for Sir Charles, I thought yet again.

Fate must have decided that he was a good man, also, for most unexpectedly Sir Charles succeeded to the title of Lord Mountjoy. Being a younger son he had never thought that he would one day be called to maintain the honour of his house, so my lady informed me one day, her black eyes ablaze with more exciting news to churn her blood.

'His father died last year, and now his elder brother, William, has died without issue, so my dearest Charles has become the new Lord Mountjoy.'

I do not know if too much of this unexpected excitement affected Lady Penelope, but for whatever reason, she did not carry her baby for as long as she should have, and this child was lost in May, before the proper time.

There was a second death in the family that year, for Lady Dorothy's husband, Sir Thomas Perrot, died in the February, leaving his wife with the one small daughter.

That summer, once my lady had recovered in health, we moved back to Essex House and I saw Lady Dorothy again.

She looked pale, and there was a tightness about her eyes and mouth which had not been present before. Perhaps her black mourning garb accentuated her pallor, but I did not think that Lady Dorothy looked well.

'I was so very sorry to hear about your sad loss, my lady,' I said, when she called me to her, and curtseyed low before her dejected form.

'Thank you, Meg, you are a dear girl as Penelope so often reminds me. I am over the worst of my grief now, and Robert has assured me that he will find another husband to comfort and protect me.'

She smiled a little forcedly.

'I do not mind being alone, and have my darling daughter, besides, to occupy my mind. But it is always a question of financial problems for us widows. The Perrot lands were forfeited due to my father-in-law's imprisonment for high treason, a felony he always denied, I may say. Now, my brother is trying to reclaim the family's estates for me, but it will all take a considerable time, I fear, thus I am grateful for a roof over my head at Essex House.'

If Lady Dorothy was in such dire straits, how could I dare to burden her further on my behalf? I took a seat beside her and remained silent, wondering why she had called for me.

'Now for you, Meg Dawlish,' she went on, more brightly. 'I have little news but will tell you what I have managed to discover since last we met.'

'Oh, my lady, I do not wish to add to your problems,' I said quickly. 'My needs are but small compared to yours, and I beg you to forget all that we discussed last year at Leighs.'

'Forget I will not!' she replied indignantly. 'I shall always endeavour to help you, Meg, in any way I can. Now, listen to me. I have found a lawyer, Master John North, who is looking into the case for you. He has ascertained that your father did indeed leave a will, and he has met the formidable Mistress Gwendoline. She will, of course, fight through every court in the land for her legal rights and, unfortunately, Master North says that the will was made out before your father remarried. It left everything to his dearly beloved daughter, Margaret.

'But as you had vanished from Cheapside and never reappeared over the years, Mistress Gwendoline was able to announce you dead. She also maintained that as she was Master Dawlish's second wife, she should rightly inherit his money and property. Now that she has seen Lawyer North, however, and heard that you are very much alive, she says that she has no objection to leaving you her possessions on her death, as she has no children.'

'But that will be in twenty, or thirty years time,' I cried, 'for I do not know how old she is but remember her as being many years younger than Father.'

Lady Dorothy nodded. 'Master North says to tell you that he will take the will to the Prerogative Court and seek to prove it for you. But he admits that Mistress Gwendoline has much right on her side. Maybe a small sum of money, or some jewels, could be passed to you now? Then at least you will possess something until you inherit everything on Mistress Gwendoline's death.'

'Please thank Master North and tell him not to bother further on my behalf,' I said. 'So much time has passed, it does not seem to be worth the trouble to engage in further legal battles.'

'But you must think of your future, Meg! I have seen what it is like to be a poor woman on her own, and my mother was in a similar state after Leicester died. Master North must insist that your stepmother makes a will in your favour, and then the comfort of old age will be secured for you.'

'Very well.' It was kind of Lady Dorothy to care about me, but it was really so unimportant being so far ahead in my life; much more important was to sort out plans for the present.

'Tell me, Meg, have you no gentleman acquaintance who might be interested in you?' asked Lady Dorothy suddenly. 'You are such a lovely girl, I would have thought some steward, or clerk at Court would have offered for you?'

The blood burned in my cheeks as I looked at her, and she knew, and smiled.

'If you do not wish to speak of it, remain silent, Meg. But may I take it that your heart does not belong to my brother?'

'Oh, indeed not, madam! I have already told you that I cannot feel warmth towards the Earl, and those feelings will never change,' I answered quickly.

'Perhaps it is just as well,' she said thoughtfully. 'We all love Robert, as you must know by now, but my mother's and my sister's emotions are considerably more involved than mine. I, at least, can see his faults and can understand what you tell me about him. But they, I fear, will never hear one word against him.'

She was so good, Lady Dorothy, so easy to talk to, so sympathetic; I wished, momentarily, that she was my mistress and not Lady Penelope. But then I would not lead the exciting, fascinating life I had now with Lady Penelope Rich, I reminded myself. For my present companion had been away from Court all her married years, and was not even wanted there now, as an impoverished widow.

'It seems to me that your sister has influenced my life in many ways,' I said, knowing that I could bare my soul to this compassionate lady, without reserve, or regret. 'A gentleman whom I have met several times both at Court, and at Chartley, would like to marry me, I believe. Although I am most fond of him, I cannot imagine living as his wife, in the countryside, and being happy with such an ordinary existence. Lady Penelope has spoilt me, you see, and I have grown to love the splendour, and the gossip, and the intrigue of both her own life, and that at Court.'

Lady Dorothy nodded as if she knew exactly how I felt. Had she, too, missed the Court after she became the wife of

Sir Thomas Perrot?

'Are you still troubled by my brother's demands?' she asked, after a moment's silence.

'Only occasionally, my lady. We were away at Leighs Priory for many months this year when I did not see him at all, and now that we are back in the Strand, the Earl appears to have forgotten about me and spends most of his time at Court.'

'Sometimes I fear for Robert's ambitious nature,' Lady Dorothy said, 'and I also feel very sorry for his wife, Frances. I wish the Queen would give him something really important to do, something really worthwhile. Then maybe his wild and tempestuous spirit would be tamed.'

She paused, allowing her dark eyes to rest thoughtfully on my face. 'As for you, Meg Dawlish, I can understand the joys of your life with Penelope, when not clouded by brother Robert, but I would bid you to have a care for the future. Perhaps it would not be a bad thing for you to marry your countryman. Then you would have somebody to protect you, you would be able to have children, with God's will, and your future would be secure. How old are you now?'

'I am twenty-seven, my lady.'

'Then do not leave it too late before you wed, although Penelope seems able to produce babies almost every year, and she is several years older than you.'

'She lost one this spring,' I replied, 'but usually she is more fortunate.'

'Some by one man and some by another,' remarked Lady Dorothy a little bitterly. 'It amazes me that Penelope can get away with so much and not be punished, though, Heaven forbid, I would not want her to experience the Queen's wrath! She is obviously a very lucky lady and it is good to see her so happy now, she suffered long enough with Lord Rich. Well, Meg Dawlish, you had best be away and help your mistress prepare herself for tonight's banquet. All I can say now is that I will keep in touch with Lawyer North and let you know what he achieves on your behalf. And spend some time thinking about the man who loves you, Meg. I have a feeling that he holds the key to your future happiness.'

Lady Dorothy held out her hand to me and as I took it in mine, and curtseyed, she drew me gently towards her and kissed me on the cheek.

The following year Lady Dorothy married for the second time, and the guests were entertained at Essex House.

I was so pleased for her, as her husband was Henry Percy, Earl of Northumberland, and I considered it to be a very fine marriage.

But my lady seemed none too sure about her sister's new husband.

'Northumberland has a hot temper,' she told me, as I dressed her hair that afternoon, 'and I fear that there will be many arguments between those two. It seems to me, Meg, that he is marrying Dorothy because he hopes that she will soon come into her rightful inheritance from the Perrot family.'

'Then why did your sister agree to marry him?' I asked. 'Surely she must have learned from your experience with Lord Rich that a marriage without love will always bring much unhappiness to the couple?'

Lady Penelope sighed. 'Dorothy needed protection,' she said, 'and Northumberland offered her that. He is also known as the 'wizard earl' and is a most learned and scholarly man, so she admires his brain. Let us hope that Dorothy will manage to give him a healthy son and heir, which is what men seem to desire above all else.'

That year of 1595 proved to be a momentous one for me, too, and my life changed dramatically, but not by marriage.

10

Towards the end of that summer, the lawyer, Master John North, whom Lady Dorothy had told me about, called to see me at Essex House. To my amazement he informed me that Mistress Gwendoline Dawlish had died from the smallpox, and that I was the sole beneficiary of the house and business in Cheapside.

'It is about time that you were able to benefit from your father's estate,' he told me gravely, a tall, thin, black-garbed man, with little humour.

But Master North was an astute lawyer and I allowed him to sort out all the documents and legal requirements on my behalf; for I was in quite a panic, not knowing how to think, how to plan, or how to act correctly with such a momentous change in my life.

In Lawyer North's capable hands

everything gradually fell into shape, and he accompanied me to Cheapside himself, and showed me around my new premises.

I must admit that I had forgotten my old home, and, after the time spent in Leighs Priory surrounded by green countryside, followed by days at Essex House in the Strand, I was somewhat disconcerted by my new residence.

The houses in Cheapside were built along a dirty street which possessed an open sewer running through the middle of it; the eaves of the houses almost touched those facing across the street, and little sunlight entered the cobbled thoroughfare.

The noise was quite dreadful to begin with, because of the coaches and carts rattling by over the cobbles, and if one was on foot the only way to avoid mud on a rainy day, or wheels over one's feet on *any* day, was to leap into the nearest doorway. However, I got used to all the inconveniences in time, and became justly proud of my new possessions.

At first it was very hard to realise that I was a lady of means, and I wished, more than once, that dear Kate Haddock was alive and that we could have experienced this delight and ownership together. But Kate was no longer here, and my Lady Penelope was unimpressed, even irritated, by my good fortune.

'But how can I manage without you, Meg?' she cried, the first time I told her my news. 'You are more, far more to me than a servant. We are friends, and have been together for the last thirteen years. And how can you hope to live in that house and run the shop all alone?'

'I have a very good adviser,' I answered. 'Master North has promised to give help and advice whenever I need it. I am retaining the present man, who organised the buying and selling of cloth under Mistress Gwendoline; he is most experienced and, I believe, trustworthy. And I have asked Mary Tredworthy, whom I have known for even more years than you, my lady, and whose father is a groom at Leighs Priory, to come to London and live with me and be my maid.'

'You? Have a maid!' She let out a spurt of laughter, but her black eyes were not amused. 'You have indeed risen above your station, Meg Dawlish. Will I have to curtsey to you next time we meet?'

'Oh, my lady,' I said, dropping to my knees and taking her unwilling hand in mine, 'let us not leave each other in bad humour. I have loved my years with you, and look upon you also as a friend, as well as mistress. Let us part company in amiable fashion, I beg, and then, if ever you should want me you have only to send word and I will come.'

'Will you really, Meg?' She stared at me in surprise, her anger fading. 'I thought that this would be the end, that we would never see each other again.'

'Only if that is what you want, my lady.' I held her long white hand to my cheek. 'I can never think of you without love, and you have only to call if you ever want me near you.'

Lady Penelope smiled then, and patted my face with trembling fingers. 'Always so good, dear Meg, and such a comfort to me. Then let us not say goodbye, but au revoir. I *shall* call for you, do not forget that. I shall want you sometimes, most urgently, as I have wanted your love and companionship in the past. So bide by what you have said, dearest Meg, and come whenever I need you.'

'I will do that,' I answered in truth, and we parted as tearfully as two separated and loving sisters.

Once I had become used to my new way of life I found great enjoyment in each day, and none of the boredom I had feared. There was a great deal to do, with supervising the cleaning and cooking by several servants, and also having to learn about the shop.

My house was blessed by a long garden at the rear of the building, some stables at the side, and the fact that it was really one large house looking like two from the front. When Lawyer North and I had entered by one door which led into the shop, with a storeroom behind it, I had wondered how I could live in such a small space after having become used to such spacious dwellings. But, to my surprise and joy, there were a further two rooms at the side which possessed their own front door. So from the street it looked like two houses side by side, but once beyond the front doors the original houses had been opened out making one large one.

So I owned two rooms at the front and two at the back on both floors, as well as two garrets beneath the eaves. The shop was at the front of one, with a storage room behind it, and the kitchen was on the other side, with a small squillerie overlooking the garden at the rear. No wonder Kate Haddock had admired the one at Leighs Priory, for my little room was just large enough to house the coal, a few brass and pewter vessels, and an assortment of kitchen herbs which had been grown in the garden.

There were two staircases, one leading up to the servants' rooms, above the shop, and the other to the rooms opposite, which had been used by Mistress Gwendoline. These would now make pleasant chambers for Mary and me, I decided. A smaller bedchamber which she and I could share, and a more reasonable sized room where we could sit together of an evening, and where we could keep our sewing and tapestry.

Mary helped me to dress and do my hair, and she and I spent many happy hours buying suitable attire; a real extravagance for me to own beautiful new gowns and shoes, and to visit a tailor, but I possessed money now and intended using it, but in a sensible way.

I also engaged another young girl, Nellie Frost, to help in the kitchen, so with the cook and the lad he already had, that made three. Rowland, my man in the shop, had two boys assisting him, so with them, and the two stable lads, there were ten mouths to feed each day. We all sat around the trestle table in the kitchen for our meals, making the evening one our main repast.

The most exciting time was when a ship was in and the horse-drawn wagons came slowly up from the river. Then Rowland and I would go out and study the sticks of hangings, the bolts of fabrics, and admire and comment on the different materials, and complain at the high prices asked.

Rowland told me that earlier Mistress Gwendoline had owned two vessels to do the trading, as my father had done, but after losing one in a great storm they had decided to sell the second. Now, different merchant ships sailed for us, as well as for other traders, and so long as we paid them a fair price for their goods, they were happy to do our business in other countries. This relieved me of the bother and cost of owning ships and having to pay the seamen.

Most of our materials came from the great Mart at Antwerp, but Master William Sheldon provided us with tapestries and wall-hangings from his weaving works in Warwick. Rowland had persuaded me to purchase carpets, also, which he had long wanted Mistress Gwendoline to do, he told me, but which idea she had always steadfastly refused. I liked the thought, however, having seen how beautifully such carpets covered the chests and tables at Whitehall Palace, and so we began a further trade with Turkey and The Levant, once the shop came into my possession.

We did a fine trade in Cheapside and I was surprised at how frequently coaches and horses pulled up outside, and both ladies and gentlemen called to examine our wares, and then to buy.

One morning, when I was busy in our back bedchamber, Mary came to call me saying that a gentleman was asking for me by name.

'I have placed him in the front room,' said Mary, and the bright look on her face puzzled me. She was a quiet girl, not often given to vivacity, and sometimes I wondered if she missed her family above the stables at Leighs Priory.

Frowning slightly, I went through to the landing and then entered the large chamber. There I saw Richard Villier standing before the fireplace, very splendid in wine-red doublet and hose, black silk stockings, and with a black velvet cloak swinging from his shoulders. On his head was a tall-crowned wine-red hat of velvet, with a feathered trim.

'Mistress Dawlish,' he bowed gracefully, 'I have found you at last.'

'How very good to see you again,' I answered, placing my hands into his outstretched ones and smiling up at his handsome face. How wonderful to meet him as an equal now, and not as a simple servant girl.

Richard looked older but attractively so, with shoulders even broader, face wider, and bearing a dark brown beard and whiskers which I had not seen before. His skin looked very healthy after the pale countenances of city folk, and his light green eyes sparkled with his old humour. He was so alive, so strongly masculine, that my heart leapt within my breast as it always did at the sight of Richard Villier.

'So, you are a woman of means now, Meg, and took my advice to beard Mistress Gwendoline in her den?'

'Not quite, sir. It was the Countess of Northumberland who did the most work, and found Lawyer North for me. Then Mistress Gwendoline, poor soul, died of the smallpox last year leaving all this to me.'

He nodded and let go of my hands. 'You are a fortunate creature, Meg, but it was time that you achieved something in your life. I did not know of all this and had some difficulty in tracing you here.'

'Why so? Did you not enquire after me at Court from Lady Penelope?'

'I saw Lady Rich but at a distance, most busily engaged in this and that. I take it the affair with Mountjoy still progresses?'

I nodded.

'It was impossible to get close to her and ask questions about you, and the various maids I did ask appeared to be new at Court and could not give me satisfactory answers. So, on I went to Essex House and eventually found a steward who could furnish me with the knowledge I needed.'

'I am so glad that you were finally successful. Will you have some wine with me, Richard? Then I will take you to examine my wares!'

'How strange to see Margaret Dawlish in a position of authority! And with servants to do her bidding.' He took off his hat and cloak and laid them on the chest which stood below the window. 'Tell me, Meg, are you happy with your new life? Is all going well with you? It looked to me as if the quality of your cloth was excellent, and I should be glad to buy some before I depart.'

'All is going extremely well, thank you, Richard, but then I am blessed with some good and hard-working servants. Yes, I am most happy here and will never regret leaving my Lady Penelope. She, naturally, was not pleased about my departure, but I have promised to go to her if ever she should have need of me.'

'To work?' asked Richard in surprise.

'No, not to work, but as a *friend*, foolish man! She might well need me to talk to, or to comfort her in some distress, and that I will gladly do. We had some very happy years together, she and I.'

Whilst we were drinking wine together Richard Villier told me that he had come to London in order to join the expedition which was shortly leaving for Cadiz.

'I have seen your erstwhile friend, Essex,' he said, with a faint smile, 'and he will be in command of the army.'

'More fighting?' I cried out. 'Will it never stop? There seems to be unending conflict in the Netherlands, and then trouble in France. Why cannot we all live in peace, sir?'

Villier shrugged. 'The might of Spain must always be feared and it is said that they are preparing a new Armada. We must attack them, Meg, before they can pounce on us.'

'You enjoy travelling to other lands, and the excitement of battle, do you not, Richard? It is hard for a woman to understand the joys of bloodshed and slaughter.'

'I do it for my country's sake,' he answered quietly, 'and also for the prizes to be gained. The Spaniards are a rich people and it is always to be hoped that either some treasure, or rich hostages, may be taken as reward.'

I did not understand such mercenary talk and was thankful to be a female, unable to take part in battle, and only occupied with my small shop's financial gains.

'Do you need more money?' I said. 'Surely the land and cattle you own in Shropshire bring you in enough? And are you not a countryman at heart — happiest in the fields and forests of your home land?'

I had never seen Richard Villier's home. It had not been a place visited by Penelope Rich and my former days were spent entirely with, and at the whim of, my mistress. But now I was an independent lady of some fair means, and if I could venture forth and visit Lady Penelope when requested, why should I not also travel further afield and see the home of my good friend Richard Villier?

I looked at his splendid, bearded face and wondered if he might ask me now that I was free to travel, and no longer bound by the chains of servitude.

Richard saw my expression and must have guessed at what I was thinking. He was always clever at reading my mind.

'Meg,' he said, 'ah, Meg. Why do I still care for you so much?' He stretched out his hands for mine once more and, grasping them firmly, pulled me up from the stool on which I sat. 'You see, my dear, life has changed for me even as it has for you. I am married now, to a sweet and gentle lady, and we have a baby son. That is the main reason for my joining Essex on his expedition, and why more money will be most welcome.'

My throat felt dry as I listened to his words, and I had difficulty in swallowing. Why had I not thought of that? Why had I always assumed that Richard Villier would be around, waiting for me forever? He had loved me, of that I was certain. And there was a time when he might have asked for my hand in marriage. That time when he told me that I possessed his heart.

'Did you get your heart back in time for the lady?' I asked huskily, still choked up inside by the shock of what he had told me. 'And what is your wife's name? And your son's?'

I must not show emotion; not sorrow, or anger, or despair at his news. I must keep bright and interested and cheerful, and be his normal, self-controlled Meg with the frozen heart.

'Her name is Maud and she is a dear, gentle girl who loves me very much. I have managed to give her a small portion of my broken heart and it keeps her happy. I needed a wife, Meg,' he went on, almost in anger, as I gazed calmly back at him. 'I needed somebody to make mine a proper home, and give me sons to inherit my land when I am gone. I waited a long time for you, Mistress Dawlish, but your Lady Penelope was of more importance than a simple country squire.'

I nodded, it was all quite understandable. Of course Richard Villier had done the right thing, and I had never wanted to be buried in the depths of the countryside, anyway.

'Tell me about your son,' I said, carefully removing my hands from his grasp and stepping back from him. 'What is he called and how old is he?'

'He is named Philip, after my best friend Sir Philip Sidney, and he is not quite one year old.'

'I am glad that you are content with your family,' I said. There was nothing else to say. 'Would you like to see some cloth now, to take back to your wife?'

Richard Villier looked at my face and shook his head, reaching for my hands again.

'Something is wrong, Meg, I can see by your lovely face which is trying so hard to remain serene. What is it, sweetheart? I cannot leave you now — after our first meeting for several years — knowing that something is amiss.'

'Nothing is wrong,' I answered, widening my eyes and forcing a smile to my lips.

Nothing that he could do anything about. It was all my own fault; such foolish, selfish actions on my part; loving the man but also loving the gay, romantic, fascinating life I led with Penelope Rich. I believed that Richard Villier would wait for me, would be patient until I had tired of my life at Court and at Essex House; would wait until I had become older, wiser, and more able to accept a country life far away from the masques, the pageants, the people and entertainments of London.

'Margaret Dawlish.' I felt his strong hands slip from mine, and suddenly my face was held hard and firm and his eyes blazed down at me, as sharp and bright as emeralds. 'Tell me the truth for once in your life. Do you love me?'

I looked into his eyes, felt his hands on my skin, and began to melt within as a mountain stream will melt, and run soft and smooth at the beginning of spring.

'Yes,' I whispered, closing my eyes and pretending no more, 'yes, I love you, Richard.'

'And about time, too!'

There was mockery in his tone, but

also joy, and his mouth came down on mine — warm, enticing, utterly irresistible. I forgot all the fear and distaste I had felt for the Earl of Essex and his unwanted embraces, and gave myself totally into the arms of the man I loved.

'This will not do,' Richard muttered, raising his head and smiling down at me. 'Where is your bedchamber? I want you, Meg, and now that you have decided to love me, I will have you!'

He bent and picked me up, my skirts billowing and puffing around his arms, but he laughed and held me tighter as one slipper fell off and rolled across the floorboards.

'Where to, Meg?' he asked.

'Through that doorway and the room at the back,' I said breathlessly. 'But, dear me, this is not right. What of the servants, and the shop? It is not yet midday. And what of your Maud?'

'Damn them all!' he cried, turning sideways and carrying me carefully through the open doorway and onto the landing. We reached the back room which I shared with Mary, and Richard deposited me upon the four-poster and then walked back to slam the door to behind him.

'The curtains will be drawn on this side,' he remarked, already beginning to draw the ones which faced the room, 'in case anyone should come venturing in.' Then he moved round to the other side of the bed which faced the window, and smiled down at me. 'But these will not be drawn because I want to see you, Meg Dawlish, see that lovely body which I have craved for so long and which has ever taunted and defied me.'

As he spoke he began undressing me, removing the outer garments with deft fingers until I was down to my shift. Then he hastily disrobed, himself, and came to me — broad-shouldered, slim-hipped, lean-thighed.

Very carefully he removed the pins and combs from my hair, then ran his big hands again and again through my locks until they slipped and slithered between his fingers. The shift was rolled back from my shoulders, and he placed his lips on my throat then down the smooth skin on my shoulders. His hands found my breasts and played and teased with the nipples, and the soft mounds of flesh, until I was crying out in ecstasy and longing for him to enter me.

'Not yet, my darling, not just yet,' he whispered, and then the shift was pulled right off my trembling body and Richard began smoothing my stomach with long, slow strokes before placing his warm mouth upon my navel.

I took his head in my hands and tugged at his thick brown hair.

'Now,' I cried out, 'take me now!'

He was harder, stronger, in every way bigger than Essex. Lady Penelope's brother was an accomplished lover but there was a softness about him, a smoothness to his flesh and a slackness of body and mouth which was not in Richard Villier. Of course, I loved the man which made everything seem better, but he was still very definitely a finer male than the idolised Earl of Essex.

Nothing hurt me now, because my body was used to it, and as I was held in the arms of the man I loved it was a joy to feel him and touch him, to want him to go on entering me and overpowering me forever. This was absolute happiness and contentment, and I knew that I could spend the rest of my days with this man, and never cease to love him.

But it was too late.

'Meg,' Richard said quietly, once we were both satisfied and lying together, bodies still entwined, his lips close to my ear. 'Meg, who was it before me?'

I held him tightly in my arms, pressing my lips against his sweat-covered shoulder.

'Essex,' I said. 'But I hated him — hated every minute of his kisses and embraces. It was never like this between us.' I lifted my head and pushed his face away from me, tugging at his beard to make him look at me. 'Do you believe me?'

Richard's eyes had darkened with anger. 'He took you against your will?'

'Essex forced me to go to him, whenever he wanted me. Often, too often, I was called to his room and there was nothing I could do save obey. I was but a servant in his house, and had always to do what he commanded.'

Richard lifted his right hand and stroked the hair back from my damp forehead. 'I warned you, Meg. I told you what would happen if you stayed with that Rich female and her selfish family. Always out for themselves, the lot of them. May their souls burn in Hell-fire at the last!'

'No.' I pushed myself up into a sitting position and stroked his chest, and his shoulders, and his curly, wet hair. 'No, Richard, let them be. Lady Penelope has been a good friend to me as well as mistress, and I will hear no ill of her. I still love her, and can never forget the years we spent together.

Good years, most of them.'

'She kept you away from me.'

'But we have had our pleasure today, my love, and Essex can no longer reach me.'

'If he tried it again,' Richard answered softly, 'without your consent I think I would kill him. You are mine, now, Meg Dawlish, and I shall not give you up — no, not even for the King of Spain!'

I laughed aloud at that and he had to smile also, then pulled me down on top of him and began making love all over again.

I am not ashamed of what happened that day with Richard Villier, or of what happened between us in the years ahead. For, from that day forth, whenever Richard was in London, he came to me and stayed in Cheapside, and my home became his for as long as he wanted.

Mary had to leave our bed and go in with Nellie Frost, but it seemed a good idea for the two girls to become friendlier, and I do not think Mary was so lonely after that.

I was very young when my father died and Mistress Gwendoline was no mother to me, but Father was a good and moral man and would not have liked the thought of his only daughter becoming mistress to a happily married man.

Kate Haddock, who never married, was an equally proper woman with strong morals and beliefs, and she would have been furious with me for my wayward behaviour.

The Queen, herself, expected all her ladies and maids at Court to remain as virginal as she was.

But I disobeyed all that I had been taught, and did what I knew in my heart to be wrong. And my only excuse was the fact that I had been too long with Lady Penelope Rich. I had seen her unhappily wed yet having to obey her husband in all things, and I had seen her loved by two good men, to neither of whom she was married. Both

Sir Philip Sidney and Lord Mountjoy adored her, and she them, and such happiness was a pleasure to behold.

When it came to me, I was only thankful that Richard Villier loved me as much as I loved him. The Earl of Essex had ruined my virginity, and could have made me hate all love-making forever. But a good man had saved me, and as long as he cared for his wife and child, and never hurt or rejected them, I could see no reason why we should not enjoy each other when the time was right.

'What if I should have a baby by you?' I said, before he left me. 'It will keep my name and I shall leave it the shop and all my money when I die. But may it be told that you are its father when it is old enough to question?'

Richard smiled. 'Of course,' he said, 'and I shall be as proud of my bastards as I shall be of my legitimate children. Be assured of that, Meg, and perhaps we can give ours a second name of Villier, so that they may know that I am not ashamed.'

'But your wife?' I said quickly. 'She must not be hurt.'

'Maud is a country girl and has never been to London, nor never will,' he answered. 'There is no reason for her ever to know about you, or a family which may one day grow up here in Cheapside.'

With that I was satisfied, and Richard left me after buying two sticks of arras hangings for the walls of his house in Shropshire. I also gave him the miniature which Master Hilliard had painted of me so many years before.

'This is a very beautiful lady,' Richard said, gazing down at the gold-framed oval in his hands, 'but it is not my Meg.'

'Then you do not want it? I am so proud of the way I look and will gladly keep it for myself.'

It was the last thing Lady Penelope had given me before I left her at Essex House, and it had been a great joy to see the miniature again for, in truth, I had quite forgotten that my lady kept it for me all those years, carefully hidden amongst her jewels.

'I shall give it to you now, Meg, for I cannot wear it back home in Shropshire,' he said slowly. 'But I will ask you for it every time I am here and will wear it at Court, and everywhere I go in London and abroad. Shortly, when we leave for Cadiz, I shall wear it most proudly, close to my heart. Remember that, and know that you are with me on my travels.'

11

I saw my Lady Penelope that year and was delighted at how well and happy she looked. She was again bearing a child by Lord Mountjoy and, as the Queen had forbidden him to take part in the expedition to Cadiz, my lady and her lover were spending a peaceful time together.

Lord Rich had gone off to join her brother, she told me, allowing them an interlude of tranquillity by themselves at Essex House.

'It is like being married at last, Meg,' she said, her eyes larger and blacker than ever in her shining face. 'Charles and I love each other so much it is always a great sorrow when we have to be parted.'

She was wearing a shorter skirt than usual, showing fine leather shoes of green with small, low heels. I thought them most elegant and decided that when I next possessed a gown, it must reach only to my ankles, and then I, too, would purchase some leather shoes.

Richard would admire them, and they would be of rose-pink, his favourite hue. Strange how everything now was thought of, planned, with Richard Villier in my mind. When Mary arranged my hair I thought of him, and which style he would most admire; my clothes were put on for him, although I knew that the moment he was in my house he would be removing my garments from my clinging body. Jewels, hats, gloves — indeed everything I put on, was worn, and chosen, with my lover in mind.

Now, I studied Lady Penelope carefully, wondering what I could learn from her and what was most admired at Court.

Her gown of green velvet was not open at the front, showing her under-dress, but was drawn in tightly at her waist in a long V-shape, and trimmed with silver ribbon at the hem, and on the bodice and sleeves. She was not showing the baby she carried in any way, and I admired her slim waist and elegant bearing. On my lady's bosom was a miniature of Mountjoy, beautifully painted by Master Hilliard, and on her golden hair was a small silk cap trimmed with the same silver ribbon as on her gown, and decorated with emeralds.

The pomander on the long gold chain which fell from her waist, smelt of rosewater, cloves and mace, and her perfumed gloves of green leather also smelt divinely.

I was very proud to be accepted as her friend, as well as her one-time servant, and showed her around my shop with pleasure. It was the first time that Lady Penelope had been to Cheapside, and she was interested in everything, and went away having bought two bolts of velvet and taffeta cloth.

My lady was content because her man remained with her, but I began to worry dreadfully about Richard. What if he should be killed in battle like his friend, Sir Philip Sidney? What if I should never see him again? And so much worse for me now to consider losing him, for we had shared our love, discussed our plans over future children, and, more important than anything else, I had lain in his arms and known true and perfect love for the first time in my twenty-nine years.

Like someone who has been starved of food, like a parched creature in the desert, I needed Richard Villier most desperately and did not know when, or even if, I would ever see his dear face again.

It was easy enough to accept Maud and little Philip in Shropshire; they had a right to him and I would always understand Richard spending more time with them than with me. Besides, I had my own servants, and my home and shop to keep me busily occupied for weeks on end. But when Richard was in Shropshire I knew where he was, that he was alive and would be travelling to see me in London when he could spare the time.

If he should die in some foreign land that would mean an end to everything; to all hopes and plans and looking forward to our future meetings. His death would be final, the absolute end to my love. Neither Penelope Rich, nor my newly-acquired possessions, could ever, in any possible way, make up for the loss of my beloved.

After seeing Lady Penelope depart, full of high spirits and glowing beauty, my mind was filled with troubled thoughts and I found it difficult to concentrate on anything save the thought of losing Richard Villier.

Foolish woman! By the end of that summer my lover had returned bringing with him some fine treasures which he had found for himself in Cadiz.

'I cannot stay long, my dearest Meg,' he cried, lifting me in his arms and swinging me around as if I were a child. 'I must return home to my family, for I have never left them alone so long before.'

'But was it worth it, Richard?' I asked, gazing at his bronzed face, and at the hair of his beard and on his head, which looked fairer, brightened by the fierce Spanish sun.

'Worth it, indeed,' he answered, and I had never seen him so excited. 'We may not like Essex, you and I, but he is a splendid leader and the men worshipped him, every one.'

'Tell me,' I said. 'Tell me quickly before you go.'

Now that I was no longer with Penelope Rich the news I received through the streets, and by traders' tongues, was often late and usually twisted and changed, so that one could never be sure if one was hearing the truth.

'Our fleet was sighted by the garrison of Cadiz at the end of June, and when the order was given to land we all went wild. Essex threw his hat into the sea, and Raleigh ordered fanfare after fanfare on the trumpets. That was *his* answer to the Spanish cannon!'

Richard lifted his sunny head and laughed aloud.

'Raleigh was there too? I thought that he was in the Tower? And he and Essex are sworn enemies, anyway.'

'There is no love lost between them, I grant you that. But both are good men and fine when they are fighting for the same cause,' Richard replied. 'The Queen had Raleigh released from prison some time ago, and his wife, Bess. I believe Raleigh is of more use to Her Majesty out of the Tower, than hidden away within its bleak walls. He most certainly played his part during this expedition. In fourteen hours the siege had collapsed and we were able to enter the city. Unfortunately, the West Indian fleet with a merchandise worth eight million crowns was hidden in the inner harbour, and before we could get at it the Spanish admiral had the entire fleet destroyed by fire.'

'You do not appear to have done badly for yourself, despite that loss,' I said. There was a new gold ring in his right ear, which I had not seen before, encrusted with diamonds, and on his doublet was pinned a heavy gold brooch, studded with pearls and emeralds.

Richard smiled and pulled me to sit upon his knee.

'I had my Meg always with me and she brought me luck.' He unbuttoned the top of his doublet and showed me the gold chain which held my miniature. 'So that you, too, have something to remember me by, I have brought some pretty trinkets for my darling.' He slipped the miniature back to fall against his chest, and then produced a little red silk purse. 'Here is a gold ring for my Meg, showing our two hands clasped together in eternal love, and these are ear-rings of best Spanish gold, with rubies set within as hearts — yours and mine.'

I thanked him and kissed him, and it was some while before he was able to continue with his tale of adventure.

'I saw Essex at his best those days in Cadiz,' he said slowly. 'He was both gallant and humane, and although we were allowed to loot where and when we chose, churches were spared and we escorted fifteen hundred monks, friars and nuns to the mainland, which chivalrous act made even the Spaniards admire him.'

'His sister, Lady Dorothy, I mean, once said to me that she wished the Queen would give Essex something worthwhile to do. Lady Dorothy admitted that her brother had many faults, but felt that much of his tempestuous and wild nature was due to his lack of achievement.'

'The Queen is not the easiest of mistresses for him,' replied Richard, rubbing his bearded chin against the side of my face. 'He asked permission to march into the interior of Spain, but

Her Majesty would not agree. Then he asked if we could put to sea and seize the next lot of returning West Indian treasure-ships, but once again the Queen refused permission. So we all returned home and yet again Her Majesty was annoyed with Essex.'

'Why so?'

'He was greeted with such jubilation by the crowds that one could almost feel he was a prince of the realm,' Richard answered, with a twisted grin, saying almost the same as I had said to Annie, at Court, some time before. 'The people are mad for him, Meg. Then in a sermon at St Paul's he was called one of the greatest generals in history, which did not please the Queen either. Lastly, she was furious because she had paid out fifty thousand pounds for the expedition, and received nothing in return.'

'But if Her Majesty had allowed you to seize the next West Indian fleet, as Essex wanted to do, you would have been able to bring back some really magnificent treasure for her, would you not?'

'We would indeed, and she disallowed such a venture. But Her Majesty is never wrong, Meg, and you must realise that. It is always somebody else who must bear the blame.'

'Hush!' I placed my hand over his teasing mouth and got soundly nipped for my action.

'Nice, sweet flesh,' he murmured, 'when may I taste some more?' and his lips went to my throat as his hand began fumbling with the buttons at my breast.

'Richard — stop! You must return home, and I was only scared in case somebody heard you speaking treason. Oh, heavens!'

Two buttons had burst, and he was tearing at the cloth and then my breasts were hanging free and in his hand and in his mouth, and his tongue was playing with my nipples making me gasp aloud in delight.

'Not here!' I was able to whisper as

he paused for breath, his eyes sparkling into mine with the gleam of a devil. 'Richard Villier, take me upstairs and do not seduce me here in the kitchen for all to see.'

'Very well, Mistress Dawlish.' He patted my torn clothing back into disastrous shape and pulled me to stand very close to him, his breath fanning my face. 'I had no intention of staying here and meant to get back to my wife and son. But I cannot leave you yet, Meg, and must have you now or I'll not sleep nights until I do! Come, entrancing wench, and join me on your bed before I lay you out over yon trestle and have my joy with you, looking like a fat pink piglet laid out for slaughter.'

'Mind your tongue, Master Villier,' I cried, slapping his bearded face.

He caught my hand and flung his other arm around my waist, then lifted me so that I hung helpless and shrieking over his shoulder.

'Lamb to the slaughter would perhaps be more flattering to a beautiful lady,' he remarked gallantly, and marched heavily up the stairs and into my chamber before throwing me upon the feather bed in a tangle of uncontrolled laughter.

I was fortunate both then, and now, in having most honest and praiseworthy servants. As soon as Mary saw Richard Villier at the house, she made herself scarce and informed all the others that he was back in our midst. Never, in all the time that Richard visited me in Cheapside, was I conscious of a servant's face in an open doorway, or footsteps or voices in an adjoining room. They all loved him, of course, for a more handsome and generous man was impossible to imagine, and, I believe, they were equally fond of me, for I tried in every way to be a good and kind mistress to them.

Our love was therefore regarded as something special, and something to be treasured, for Richard came none too frequently to Cheapside. When he did, we were definitely spoiled and encircled by an invisible wall which gave us complete protection in our little oasis of private joy.

The year of 1597 was another tumultuous one for Lady Penelope and although I did not live with her any longer, I remained true to my word and went to see her whenever she asked.

She wanted me to be present at the birth of her first son to Lord Mountjoy, so I visited Essex House for the first time that January, since I had left it.

Fortunately, I did not see Robert Devereux, the Earl of Essex, for he was at Court the few days that I remained with my lady, but I saw Lord Mountjoy again, and what a proud and happy man he was when his son was placed in his arms.

The delighted parents christened the boy Mountjoy, although he took the second name of Rich, as his sister, Penelope, had done. I thought it both strange and dangerous that they should so openly declare their love for all the world to see. But, once again, Lord

Rich accepted the situation, and I remembered my Richard's words to me and knew that if I should have a babe, we would do exactly the same and use the name Villier at the baptism ceremony.

Yet, I thought, we were not well-known people, and of little consequence to the world at large, whereas Lady Penelope was sister to the Earl of Essex, and Lord Mountjoy stood high in the Queen's regard.

I could only watch and pray, hoping that no evil spirit would cause harm to any of them.

In the April of that year I received a pathetic letter from my lady informing me that she was suffering from the smallpox, and that both she and Lord Rich were staying at St Bartholomews, his London house, in Smithfield.

She told me that she was feeling very low and depressed, bade me not to visit her for fear of infection, but to send her news of the outside world.

. . . 'I feel so alone here and yet so

ugly that I would not wish anyone to see me in my disfigurement. With God's help I shall recover and perhaps regain some of my former beauty. If such a miracle is possible? If not, you will have to come to me and paint my face in the manner we once discussed so long ago. Tell me of the Court, Meg, if you should hear word of it. And what news of my brother? I hope that he behaves himself before the Queen, and worry greatly at his foolish handling of money. Would that he could pay off all his debts and begin his life afresh! . . . '

My poor lady, it seemed to me as if she worried more about her reckless brother than she did about herself. There was little I could tell her, unfortunately, being at Court no more and having seen nothing of Richard Villier for some time, who always seemed to know everything about Court gossip and happenings.

I did write and beg her to put red cloth up against the windows of her bedchamber, for I remembered that

Kate Haddock had always told me that if I should ever catch that dread disease, a red cloth, or petticoat, keeping out the light, was a wondrous way of stopping the awful scarring of the smallpox.

Lady Penelope assured me that she was taking my advice, and it was a joy to see her that summer, at Essex House again, and fully recovered with no blemish upon her fair white skin.

In July her lover, and brother, and Lord Rich, all sailed off on the Islands Voyage, and I went to see my old mistress on several occasions for she was missing Lord Mountjoy and, to my concern, was with child once more. Although physically quite mended, Lady Penelope was in a fretful state of mind for the news about the English fleet was not good.

'My brother was told to sail to the Islands and destroy the Spanish treasure fleet there,' she told me.

'What islands?' I asked, very aware of how little I knew.

'There is a small group of islands, a thousand miles off the Spanish coast, where the ships which carry treasure from the silver mines in Peru to Madrid, anchor to rest and reprovision themselves. Charles gave me a lesson about them before he sailed, and the task set for my brother seemed easy enough, Meg.'

'But?' I queried, seeing by the look on her worried face that all was not going well for the Earl of Essex and his fleet.

'But they were beset by bad weather and terrible storms; there have been arguments and disagreements between Robert and that wretch, Raleigh, so I have been told at Court, and they have not even *seen* a Spanish vessel, let alone captured one. And it is September already,' she ended dully.

My lady looked so miserable that I arose from my stool and went to put my arms around her.

'Do not worry yourself about them any more,' I said softly. 'There is nothing you can do to help matters, and you should be giving all your thoughts to your unborn child.'

Lady Penelope nodded, then smiled slightly before putting up one hand and patting my arm.

'Dear Meg, I do miss not having you with me every day. I miss that calm good sense and gentle voice of yours. Come and see me often, please, whilst Charles and Robert are so far away.'

I assured her that I would and, indeed, managed two more visits before the men she loved returned from their Islands Voyage. They returned, however, without joy or plunder, and the Queen was angry with the Earl of Essex for squandering so much of her money. Apparently, there was a heated argument at Court and then Essex went off to his house in Wanstead, to sulk.

Everything must have been sorted out eventually, and tempers cooled, for Essex returned to London and my lady told me in a long letter filled with love and admiration for her Robin, that the

Queen had bestowed the title of Earl Marshal of England on Robert Devereux.

After the fleet returned towards the end of October, Lady Penelope had a few precious weeks of happiness with Lord Mountjoy, but when their second son was born he did not live for long. This was small wonder to me for she had borne him during her weeks of sickness, and her body could not have been in a strong condition so soon after little Mountjoy's birth.

This third child by Lord Mountjoy was named Scipio and baptised on the 8th December at Essex House, shortly before he died.

From that time on the years became more and more turbulent for Lady Penelope, and I shared much of the grief and anxiety with her, for although we no longer lived together I always loved her, and could not forget the many years we had spent in each other's company.

Apart from her brother, I knew that

my lady also had problems with her mother, for the Countess of Leicester, as she remained despite her third marriage to Sir Christopher Blount, kept imploring both her beloved Robin, and her daughter, to use their influence to get her back to Court.

On one occasion the Earl of Essex was almost successful. In the spring of 1598, Lady Penelope told me of what happened, and I would have laughed had my lady not looked so upset by the tale.

'Mother came up to London to join us in a St Valentine Day's party,' she said, 'and begged Robert to speak to the Queen and allow her to see her, whilst she was up from the country.'

I nodded, wondering what was to happen next to the determined Lettice.

'It was all arranged that Her Majesty would meet Mother at Tilt End, and we had all put some money together so that a splendid gift of a jewel, costing three hundred pounds, was awaiting the Queen in Mother's trembling hands.'

'Was Her Majesty pleased with the gift?' I asked, knowing how much the Queen adored gems, and all kinds of finery.

'She did not come!' cried Lady Penelope. 'Her coach was all ready to take her to Tilt End and she changed her mind. Poor Mother was beside herself with grief, and the waste of precious money, so Robert said he would speak to the Queen in private.'

'And?' I hardly dared to ask further.

'The Queen promised him that she would receive Mother at Court next day. This she did, and they both embraced and Mother kissed hands — but that was the end of it, Meg. So much Her Majesty will do for Robert, but she quite refuses to have Mother at Court and says that is now the end of the matter. *So* disappointing, and Mother has returned to the country in great distress.'

I did not like to ask what had happened to the jewel, but I thought even less of the Countess of Leicester after that. Why could she not accept her present life, and the fact that the Queen would never like her? It seemed so foolish, and so humiliating to me, that a lady could keep on begging for something she must *know* she could not have. But so long as her adored Robin, and her daughter, Penelope, were enjoying Court life, Lettice, Countess of Leicester, obviously would not be happy until she could take part in the entertainments, and the glory, also.

Richard Villier was the first to warn me of the gathering storm, as we lay in bed after an afternoon of love. He was in London for several days, on business at Court, and he spent as much time with me as possible. They were precious hours for us, for sometimes he remained in Shropshire for months at a time and I was never certain how long it would be before I saw him again.

'I believe your Lady Rich has some influence on her spoilt brother,' Richard said against my shoulder, his beard tickling my warm flesh. 'If you should see her in the near future, bid her tell her beloved Robin to have a care.'

'What has he done now?' I asked sleepily, still lazy from love-making.

'He has angered the Queen greatly and I fear does not fully comprehend the danger.'

'But Essex is always angering the Queen,' I retorted, 'and she always forgives him.'

'So he believes. But there will come a time when Her Majesty has had enough of that young man, and I have a feeling that the time is not far off.'

I shifted in Richard's arms, turning my head to look more closely at his face. 'Tell me what happened,' I said.

'It is all the talk of Court at present and nobody is quite certain which way the tide will turn. At a meeting of the Privy Council Essex contradicted the Queen and then turned his back on her.'

'Oh, no!' Such an insult would never be forgiven.

'Worse was to follow, apparently. Her Majesty was outraged and boxed his ears, telling him to go and be hanged. To which Essex replied that he would not have borne such an outrage from her own father's hands, and reached for his sword.'

'Good God in Heaven!' I clapped my fingers over my mouth and stared at Richard, feeling as if my eyes would pop from my head. 'He is a fool — a damned, stupid fool! Was he not sent to the Tower for that?'

'No. The Lord Admiral restrained him from drawing his sword, the Queen stood rigid, and there was complete silence in the chamber. Then Essex broke away from the group and ran out of the room. He has retreated to his country home in Wanstead and the Queen has not spoken of the matter again.'

'My poor lady,' I said, running my fingers through my tousled hair, 'I wonder if she knows? Doubtless the news has reached her but I had best write and offer comfort. She always worries so much about that wretch. Why can she not see that he brings all the troubles upon himself?'

Richard shrugged, then pulled me down into his arms again.

'Forget Devereux and your beloved Penelope, and give me more of your love, Meg Dawlish. Later, when I am gone, you may write your letter of comfort, or warning, or what you will.'

★ ★ ★

In September I received another letter from Lady Rich. She thanked me for my condolences and said how greatly she cherished my friendship.

... 'I have a request for you now, dear Meg, and hope so much that you will agree to it. Will you not come down to Leighs and join us in this miserable corner of the world? I have another dear friend with me, called Elizabeth, whom I would like you to meet. We are both low in spirit and I believe your good sense and comfort will give us both hope for the future. Come and stay a while, dearest Meg, if you can spare your old mistress and friend some precious hours of your time . . . '

Naturally I could not refuse her and wanted to know the latest news of her, and her family, besides. I had been linked with the Devereux family for so long that whatever befell them, whatever pleased or worried them, must always have some effect upon me, also.

This proved to be a good opportunity to take Mary with me. She had not been back to Leighs Priory since I had taken her to work for me in Cheapside, so I felt that the journey to Essex would give her the chance to visit the rest of the Tredworthy family, and allow her a pleasant few days back in the countryside she loved.

For the first time in my life I was treated as an honoured guest at Leighs, being given my own chamber on the west side of the house, and a maid to care for my needs whilst Mary stayed with her family above the stables.

Fortunately my gowns were now of good quality and design, and I had begun to buy jewellery for myself, as well as owning the gold ring and the gold and ruby ear-rings which Richard had given me. Best of all was the fact that I now wore a ruff every day. It was only a small one, nothing like the double ruffs, the lace-edged ones, the pearl-encrusted ones, or the beautiful lace-edged wing collars which my lady often wore in place of a ruff. It was neither extravagant, nor bejewelled, but gave me enormous confidence. Now that I was a lady of means, and Father had been a well-educated and intelligent man, I felt it was quite in order for me to wear a ruff, so long as it was in a modest, unpretentious fashion.

So, reasonably attired, I did not feel too out of place beside Lady Penelope and her friend Elizabeth, Countess of Southampton.

Poor ladies, it was no wonder that they felt depressed, shut away in that vast mansion set in its acres of parkland, and with no entertainments or gay companionship.

My Lady Penelope had just produced her third son by Lord Mountjoy, named St John, and the Countess of Southampton was heavy with child, due in November. All their friends were in London, and at Court, and here they were buried in austere and puritanical Leighs Priory.

'It is pleasant for me to be with another lady who has not abided by the rules,' said Lady Penelope, as we sat together that first afternoon of my visit. 'Poor Elizabeth has behaved very badly in Her Majesty's eyes, although fortunately for her, the Queen has taken out her wrath on Henry, not his wife this time.'

I liked Elizabeth at once and saw humour in her blue eyes which was always a most useful quality to possess, particularly if one was involved with the Devereux family. I realised that I also knew her husband, for he was the Earl of Southampton, patron of Will Shakespeare, whom I had seen on occasion at Essex House.

'It was not entirely our fault, Meg,' explained the Countess calmly. 'Henry did in fact ask for the Queen's permission for us to wed, because I was a maid of honour and we felt that Royal Permission was most necessary. However, Her Majesty refused and told Henry to travel abroad for two years.'

'You were supposed to forget him during that time,' said Lady Penelope, 'and continue with your attendance on the Queen until *she* found you a husband.'

The Countess of Southampton gave a wry smile.

'But,' went on my lady, 'the Queen is a virgin, and really has no idea which person is best suited for another. Look how my marriage was approved by everybody, yet what a disaster it turned out to be!'

'You have been a good wife, madam,' I put in quickly, 'for you always come when Lord Rich calls, and you have given him the sons he most wanted.'

'I have been a good wife,' Lady Penelope agreed, 'but they were miserable years for me. You must remember, Meg? It is only now that I have found true happiness and contentment, and the man I love is not my husband!'

'What of the Countess?' I turned to smile at my lady's companion. 'I presume you wed without Royal Consent?'

'Henry went dutifully off to France to begin his travels and it was then that I discovered I was bearing his child.' She reached out her hand and touched Lady Penelope's arm. 'Both Essex and Penelope have been wonderful to me,' she said softly. 'Essex had Henry brought back from France and we were married secretly at Essex House. Then my dearest husband returned to the continent and Penelope invited me to stay with her until the birth of my child.'

'It must be a comfort for you both to

be together with your babies,' I said.

'But the Queen has found out and Henry has been brought back to England and imprisoned in Fleet Prison,' cried Elizabeth.

'Do not worry,' replied my lady firmly. 'Robert will secure Southampton's release, and I know he has had some rooms set aside for you both in Essex House.'

'Henry and your Robert have long been friends,' answered the Countess, 'but I pray that the Queen will not hold this kindness against Essex. He does not seem to be in so high a favour these days.'

Lady Penelope glanced across at me and shrugged her shoulders. 'I have heard that Robert does not always please Her Majesty, and I have warned him several times to be careful. However, he is such a charmer I do not believe the Queen's anger will ever last for long against him.'

I remembered Richard's words to me and I wondered. But I had done all that was possible to warn Lady Penelope, and she had far more contact at Court than me. Lord Mountjoy, too, was often in the Royal Presence, having recently been created Knight of the Garter by Her Majesty, and he must be constantly aware of what was going on. He was in the best position to listen, then to advise Lady Penelope. I could do no more.

12

1599 was a black year, and Richard Villier warned me to keep well clear of Lady Penelope Rich and to remain busily occupied with my shop in Cheapside. He came up to see me for a few days that summer, and his face was unusually grave as he gave me news of the Earl of Essex.

'He was sent to Ireland against the Queen's will, but he insisted that he was the right person for the post of Lord Deputy of Ireland, and Her Majesty gave in to his demands.'

'I knew that he had gone,' I said. 'My lady wrote to me from Chartley and told me the news. She was so hoping that her brother would make a success of this appointment — he is most terribly in debt, I believe, and needs huge sums to clear his financial problems.'

'Essex will clear no debts this way,' answered Richard grimly. 'He is making mistake after mistake and creating his own downfall. He has taken the Earl of Southampton with him and made him Master of Horse, which the Queen expressly forbade; she is still angry with Southampton for marrying against her will and although she allowed his release from prison, she is not happy about the close friendship between him and Essex.

'Essex has been giving out far too many knighthoods, which angers Her Majesty even more, and it is now reported that he has been unable to bring down the Irish rebel, Tyrone, and so has made a truce with him, instead.'

'Dear me, he seems to be doing nothing right at present.'

'The Queen is furious,' said Richard.

'What will Essex do now? Will he dare to return to England? Or will he stay in Ireland and try to improve his position?'

Richard put his arms about me and

held me close to his broad chest.

'I beg you to keep away from the Devereux family, Meg,' he said against my hair, and I could feel his heart thumping through the satin padding of his doublet. 'I am fearful of what Essex plans next. It is said that his stepfather, Sir Christopher Blount, who is also with him, is trying to make him refrain from violence. But the hot-headed Southampton is urging him on. There is an ugly rumour going around that Essex will decide to bring his army back, to march on London.'

I bit at my bottom lip and clung to Richard, feeling sick with fury. I did not care about Robert Devereux — to my mind he had brought all this trouble upon himself and deserved punishment — but I did care about his sister. And, knowing my lady as well as I did, it was obvious to me that Lady Penelope would stand by her brother no matter what danger there might be for herself, supporting him in anything, and everything, he might do.

Fortunately for my peace of mind, I heard later from my lady that Essex had returned to England with but a few friends, and had ridden straight to see the Queen at Nonsuch Palace, to try and explain his acts of disobedience.

Unfortunately, from Robert Devereux' point of view, he had ridden to Court at great speed and had burst in upon the Queen unannounced.

'There at Nonsuch,' Lady Penelope told me in a hushed voice, 'he saw Her Majesty without her wig, in a state of undress, and with no make-up on her face, or jewellery. She allowed Robert to kiss her hand, and she listened to him calmly and sweetly. But it was a foolish, thoughtless thing for him to do — *no* female likes to be seen in such naked disarray and particularly not when she is old, and vain, and the Queen of England!'

'What happened then?'

'She sent Robert off to get washed and changed, and when he saw her later in the day she appeared less sympathetic towards him. Then, that night, Meg, he was ordered to keep to his chamber.'

Lady Penelope stopped talking and placed one hand to her brow.

'And now?' I asked softly, knowing that she would have to tell me everything, that it was good for her to talk, good to share her anxieties with another person. It was useless for Richard Villier to warn me about the Devereux family and bid me leave them be; I could no more desert Penelope Rich than I could have deserted Kate Haddock in trouble, when she was alive. Though unconnected by blood, they were both my family and I would always support them, through good or bad times, until, like with Kate, death parted us.

I leaned forward and took Lady Penelope's hand in mine, feeling her long white fingers cold to my touch.

'Tell me,' I said.

'Robert is now at York House, home of the Lord Keeper, and he is imprisoned there, Meg, and not even allowed to see Frances, or the baby daughter she has recently borne him.'

For the next few months my lady was in a restless and distracted state of mind, not staying in any one place for any length of time but continually travelling, from Court to Leighs Priory, from Leighs to Chartley back to Leighs again and then on to Wanstead, to prepare her brother's home there to which he was not allowed to return.

She produced another son for Lord Mountjoy that year, and he was baptised Charles, and to my relief the baby proved to be healthy despite his mother's continual travels and anxieties.

Towards the end of that year Lady Penelope begged me to join her and bring my usual 'comfort and good sense' with me. But this once I refused. For one thing I had Christmas and the New Year's celebrations to think about, and wanted to give my good servants a happy time. And another reason was the fact that my lady was not alone; she had the Countess of Southampton with her, her sister, Dorothy, now the Countess of Northumberland, as well as her mother, Lettice, and sister-in-law, Frances.

I felt that my presence amongst all these ladies was really not necessary and knew, also, that they would be talking and crying about Essex all the time, which would have aroused my anger somewhat more than my sympathy.

Richard did not join me over the festive period, but he wrote several times and, apart from his words of love which were always a joy to read, he also kept me informed on Court matters.

Once, I had jokingly told him that I believed he must have spies at Court, and he had answered quite seriously that he had.

'Not spies as Walsingham possessed so efficiently,' he said, 'but I have an agent who keeps his eyes and ears open for me and sends any information which he feels may be of interest.'

'I wondered how you always knew so much — but is it really necessary?' I asked, somewhat perplexed.

'Everything that happens at Court is of importance, Meg, for it is the hub of our small universe, and one must always be aware of what the Queen is planning. Posts and appointments may fall vacant, and expeditions planned — all of which might suit me and bring more money into my ever demanding coffers. I have told you before, Meg, and will say it again — *everybody* needs financial gain in their lives, and it is most important to have prior knowledge of rewarding events.'

Such thinking and organising was beyond me, but then I lived in London and people from Court often came to my shop and bought lavishly, making sure that my future was secure.

Richard, of course, lived far away in Shropshire and would have no knowledge of Court matters unless he kept an agent on the spot, to send him news whenever it might benefit him.

Why the Earl of Essex should be of such interest to Richard Villier I did not know, except that he had been the Queen's favourite for some time, and doubtless the vultures were gathering in order to snatch what they could, should he fall from grace.

Also, more charitably, I knew that Richard was concerned about me and my involvement with the Devereux family, therefore he no doubt also made it his business to find out all he could about Essex, to pass on the news to me should I not have heard already from Lady Penelope Rich.

Early in December he wrote to tell me that the Earl of Essex was very ill.

. . . 'I believe his lodgings at York House are very confined, and he has been ill for some time and shows no sign of improvement . . . I have heard that Lady Rich and Lady Northumberland have appeared at Court dressed all in black, and in this mourning garb they hope to draw the Queen's attention to their request. They want Essex to be allowed to return to his own home, but up until now Her Majesty has ignored their pleas . . . '

He also told me that the Queen had appointed Mountjoy Lord Deputy of Ireland, to take the place of Essex.

Early in March I heard from him again, telling me that Lettice, Countess of Leicester, was up to her old tricks and pestering Her Majesty again.

. . . 'if the Countess only knew, she is probably annoying the Queen more than ever, for now it is said that she purchased a gown for Her Majesty, which must have cost at least one hundred pounds. This was sent to Court but the Queen neither accepted, nor refused it. It is obvious that the lady is very worried about her adored son, and wants to see the Queen and beg for his release — but I do not think, dear Meg, that Her Majesty will ever take notice of the mother of the Earl of Essex! . . . '

On the 22nd March, Robert

Devereux, who had by then recovered from his illness, was allowed to return to his own home, but under house-arrest. Then I heard, to my horror, that Lady Penelope had written several letters to the Queen on her brother's behalf, naming some of her brother's enemies, and warning that once they had disposed of Robert, they would then turn on the Queen, herself.

One of these letters, without my lady's consent, had been printed and made public, and because of this Lady Penelope was confined to her husband's London home of St Bartholomews, in Smithfield.

I immediately went to try and visit her there but was informed that she had gone to Barn Elms. This was where her sister-in-law, Frances, often stayed, so I hurried there, in the hope of seeing my lady and finding out what was happening to her.

To my surprise and joy she was there, and quite cool and confident, dressed in a beautiful gown of peach-coloured satin, with a lace-edged wing collar at her neck, falling to a V at her breast. She wore no ruff but a solid gold necklace in its place, with a huge ruby set in the centre. There was a wide pleated peplum of peach satin, edged with velvet ribbon, resting upon her farthingale, and her fine leather shoes were made of a peach fabric and trimmed with gold rosettes. I had never seen her looking so lovely, and so magnificently attired.

Lady Penelope hurried towards me and put both arms around me, no doubt crushing her satin gown but not caring in her pleasure at seeing me again.

'Why, Meg, you are shivering,' she cried, stepping back but still holding my hands in hers, 'are you not well?'

'I am quite well but most dreadfully worried,' I answered. 'I did not know where you had gone to and heard that you were under house-arrest, like your brother.' It was still hard to believe that she was here, and alive, and in such good spirits.

'Penelope always manages to find her way out of danger,' said Frances, her pale face looking thin and drawn, and obvious fear for her husband showing in her eyes.

'I have been questioned by the Lord Treasurer and my answers were found to be both sincere and repentant,' answered my lady firmly.

'But what made you write such dangerous words?' I cried, looking into her animated, lovely face which showed none of the strain of her sister-in-law's countenance. Yet she must be worried, too, about her beloved Robin. What saved Lady Penelope, I thought suddenly, was the fact that she was *doing* something. She was actively engaged in writing letters, thinking of ways and means, planning and plotting. Lady Penelope Rich could never sit quietly, miserably at home, doing nothing, like her pathetic sister-in-law.

'What names did you pass on to the Queen?' I asked, trying to calm myself in the face of her confidence. 'You will have made terrible enemies now, my lady, and they will endeavour to wreck your life, as much as they will your brother's.'

'The Queen has pardoned me for writing so much, although she was displeased about the publication of one of my letters. However, she now realises that this was done without my knowledge, or my consent.'

'Was the one that was published the letter which bore those names?'

'No, Meg dear, that one reached her eyes only, Her Majesty has assured me, and was then destroyed.'

'Thank God for that,' I said.

'Let us hope that the Queen was not mistaken,' broke in Frances softly, 'for Robert Cecil has eyes everywhere, and is often with Her Majesty. I would not put it past that little cripple to glance at some of her private papers, without Her Majesty's knowledge.'

'Then he will have seen that I warned of him,' said my lady, her black eyes smouldering. 'Cecil, Bacon and Raleigh are the three who are out for my brother's blood.'

'But *you* are safe?' I said swiftly, not wanting to hear any more about Essex and his enemies. 'The Queen has forgiven you and allowed you your freedom?'

Lady Penelope nodded. 'Her Majesty has pardoned me and I shall go to Leighs tomorrow. My husband is not well and requires my presence there, to nurse and comfort him.' She paused, and the corners of her mouth turned down. 'Now that Charles is away in Ireland, and Robert remains under house-arrest, there is no reason why I should not go to Leighs Priory. I shall see my children again, which will be a joy, and I shall take Elizabeth with me and Frances, also, if she desires it.'

'Then take care,' I begged, 'and remain at Leighs Priory for as long as you can. It is surely a safer and better place for you at present.'

Lady Penelope nodded her golden

head and kissed me most affectionately before I took my leave of her; but I knew that her thoughts were still mainly on her brother, and that she would stay away from London for as short a time as possible. My lady did not relish danger, but she loved intrigue as I had always known, and to her, excitement and thrills were always bound up with her reckless brother Robert.

There followed a blessed period of tranquillity and, whilst at Leighs, Lady Penelope gave birth to her last child, another daughter for Lord Mountjoy, named Isabella.

At the end of August the Earl of Essex was released from house-arrest and told that he could go anywhere except to Court. He went first to Chartley to rest and regain his strength, I heard later from Richard, but soon began to pester the Queen with letters. He was more deeply in debt than ever, and was relying on Her Majesty to renew the lease of the sweet wines, the monopoly of which he had taken over after the Earl of Leicester's death.

'But,' Richard told me, on his visit to London before the Christmas of 1600, 'the Queen has refused to renew his grant. The annual value is, I believe, about fifty thousand pounds, for which Essex would have been more than grateful. But Her Majesty has decided that the monopoly will now belong to the Crown.'

'Everything appears to be going badly for him,' I said, almost feeling sorry for the man. 'At one time I hated him, for he used me most cruelly and yet could do no wrong in anyone else's eyes.'

'Except for mine.' Richard kissed me tenderly on my mouth. 'For he had experienced my Meg before me — and I was both angry and jealous.'

'Yet now we are the fortunate ones, for we have love and satisfaction and great joy, and Robert Devereux is left with — what?'

'He is in very great trouble, for now that the Queen no longer favours him, his creditors are demanding instant payment, and he has lived on debts for most of his life.'

'And whilst he was Court favourite they did not matter?' I remembered the orange and white army which he had paid for so lavishly to escort him to France.

'Whilst Essex was with the Queen he could do anything, ask for anything, and all was allowed him because he was favourite. Now those debts must be paid, and the Earl of Essex is penniless. He has, in fact, but one thing left.'

I looked at Richard in surprise. 'What is that?'

'He has a sister who will do anything he asks of her — and he is asking much, Meg.'

'What do you mean?' I saw a grim expression on Richard's face and felt the familiar churning in my stomach when fear possessed me. What was to happen now?

'You will not like this but now *I* am asking something. Will you return with me to Shropshire?'

'Shropshire?' Stupidly I repeated the word, not understanding what was going on at all. Had his Maud died? Was he going to ask me to marry him? And what had Shropshire to do with Essex and his present misfortunes?

'You cannot come to my home, much as I should like that, but a place could be found for you on my estate, and I want you out of London for the next few months. What say you to a peaceful sojourn in the countryside?'

Richard smiled as he spoke, then bent to kiss the tip of my nose, but his eyes were bleak — a cold grey-green, like the frosted fields of winter.

My heart eased its sudden pounding, and my stomach calmed at his words. I pulled a little away from him.

'This has something to do with my lady, has it not? You are always trying to separate us and I know you too well by now, Richard Villier.'

It was not his wife's death, nor a hope of marriage. It was danger, and in some way it was connected with Lady Penelope Rich.

Richard sighed and pulled me close to his chest.

'I do not know when you last heard from Lady Rich, but she has returned from Leighs Priory and both she and her brother are now at Essex House. They are plotting together, Meg, with some of Essex's best friends and supporters. Lady Rich, herself, is going about trying to summon up as many men as possible to support her brother's cause, and his secretary, Henry Cuffe, is gathering together all the disaffected who see Essex as their salvation. I, too, have been contacted and that is why I leave for Shropshire tomorrow — I will have none of it.'

'But what do they intend doing?' My throat was dry. The last time something like this had happened, when Essex was in Ireland, he had returned with but a few friends and ridden to see the Queen to seek her understanding. 'Does he intend seeing the Queen again?' I asked. 'Even though he has been banished from Court. Does he intend taking a group of friends and support-ers and demanding financial aid?'

'I think he is mad,' answered Richard slowly, 'but I believe he will march on London, summon the City to back him, and then advance on the Court. He wants Cecil and Raleigh gone, maybe even the Queen, and will take all power into his own hands. Some are saying that he has the crown of England in his heart. It is the only certain way for him ever to get his hands on some money again.'

'He is crazed. Such a thing is not possible. No one will support him in such a devilish act!'

'It has been done before, Meg. Richard the Second was deposed by Henry Bolingbroke, as one of Will Shakespeare's plays shows at South-wark. Oh, yes, it can be done and Essex has many supporters. Raleigh and Cecil are hated by some, there is too much power in the wrong hands, the Queen is old, and James of Scotland is unknown here. Whereas Essex is a young and attractive man and adored by the crowds.' He leaned forward and put his hands to his head. 'God alone knows what will happen, Meg, and who will be victor, but I am not staying a day longer in this seething pot of treason, and will go to the country tomorrow. All I ask is, will you come with me?'

I looked at his dear face now turned towards me, and at his caring eyes and loving hands. If Richard Villier were a free man, I would go with him anywhere he asked, whenever he asked. But he was married to Maud and there was no place for me in his home.

The thought of some damp, ill-kept lodging amongst strangers, who might resent my uninvited presence, daunted me. Here was my home, my servants, my work, and my lady might yet have need of me. I could not imagine that I would ever be in danger, for I was a nobody. But Lady Penelope might be made to suffer and, if so, I wanted to be near her.

'Dearest Richard,' I answered softly, 'I love you and you must know that well enough by now. But I also like my independence and cannot imagine hiding myself away in the country when something of great importance may be happening here, on my doorstep. I have good and loyal servants, and fear no one. So no, I will not journey with you on the morrow. Do not forget me, please, and once these turbulent days are over come back and visit your Meg again.'

He was not happy with my answer and was loth to leave me in Cheapside, but the following day he returned to Shropshire and I did not see him again.

13

What followed will, I suppose, pass down in history.

Living in Cheapside I saw the cavalcade that Sunday, on the 8th February, led by Essex, come thundering down from Lud Gate Hill, followed by several hundred men on foot, and I heard Essex calling at the throng who had gathered for the morning's sermon at St Paul's Cross, to join him.

He shouted out that Raleigh was trying to murder him.

'A plot is laid for my life!' I heard him yell. And further — 'Cecil has planned to give the throne of England to Spain!'

I saw Sir Christopher Blount, also, the husband of Lettice, marching at the head of a small group of rebels, a few of them carrying halberds in their raised arms, and he was shouting and calling, trying to entice more men to join the excited mob.

But, from the upstairs window, I could see how many people looked, cheering and waving from doorways and windows, yet people who appeared strangely unmoved by the once-great Essex. They seemed to find the scene more of a Sunday outing, a pageant arranged for their benefit, not a desperate attempt to seize the Crown. And, noticing how few were on horseback, how few were properly armed, I realised that this was a badly organised, poorly planned rebellion.

Suddenly, my fear and hatred of Robert Devereux vanished, and I could feel nothing but pity for him, and a terrible ache of sadness in my breast.

Whilst Essex and his supporters were engaged in trying to raise the disinterested City to arms, the Privy Council acted. Robert Cecil's brother was sent out into the streets with a Royal Proclamation denouncing Essex as a traitor, and promising pardon to all his followers who would desert him.

'That is the end for him now, mistress,' murmured Rowland beside me.

We were all pressed against the upper window, watching and hearing, but keeping ourselves carefully behind locked doors. Mary was weeping at my side, and one of the shop lads was rubbing his eyes with a dirt-engrimed fist.

Richard had been right, I thought, there had been a magic in Robert Devereux, Earl of Essex; a charm, a romantic illusion which had brought him close to rich and poor, alike. But he had not used his good qualities to his own advancement, and had made too much of his arrogance, his hot-tempered whims, his lack of judgement. He had put too much trust into the hands of a selfish, vain, yet all-powerful Queen. And what of his friends? I remembered the clever, serpent-eyed Francis Bacon at Essex House; how he had lived with Robert Devereux and spent hours, days, in his company, he, and his brother, Anthony. Yet now, it was said, Francis Bacon had gone over to the other side and had become a tool of Robert Cecil's.

As we stood waiting, unable to drag ourselves away from the window, unable to think, or talk, or remember anything save for that band of rebels led by a handsome, thoughtless, impossible man, we heard a clatter of hooves once more and a smaller, less enthusiastic, weary band came into view. I could see the sweat on Essex's desperate face, and on his stained doublet, and there was fear on the faces of many. They rode and marched back in the direction of Lud Gate Hill and the Strand, and I wondered, bleakly, what would become of them all.

Later, I heard that Essex had returned to his house by river, and barricaded himself in until the Queen's soldiers arrived and he was made to surrender.

Once the streets had cleared and I

felt it was safe to venture out, I took Mary with me for support and went to Essex House. There were soldiers everywhere, and we had great difficulty in getting through, but eventually a distraught steward informed me that the Earl of Essex and his chief supporters were confined in the Tower.

'And Lady Rich?' I asked.

Why was she not present? What had happened to her? Was my lady in the Tower, also? Mary held my hand tightly as I waited for a reply.

'Lady Rich has been put in the custody of the Keeper of the Privy Purse,' we were told.

Hastily we went further, Mary and I, and found the home of Henry Sackford, Keeper of the Privy Purse. At first we were not allowed to enter, but at last I found a friendly guard who escorted me to my lady, whilst Mary was ordered to wait outside in the courtyard.

What did they think, those foolish men? That we possessed cannon and gunpowder hidden beneath our clothing? That swords and daggers lay underneath our skirts? That we, small and fragile women, would attack the men of that household?

No matter. Within the hour I was shown into a chamber where Lady Penelope was imprisoned.

She gasped, cried out, then clutched me to her as if she would never let me go.

'Meg, oh, my dearest Meg — I cannot believe that someone has at last come to me! Put your arms around me, darling, and hold me tightly. I have been so alone and so very worried. Tell me, what passes beyond these walls? And what has become of Robert?'

I told her that I knew nothing as yet, but would try to find out all possible news before seeing her again.

'I had first to find out where you lay, and if you were all right, my lady,' I said, drawing back from our embrace and looking closely at her.

Her hair was tangled and but roughly

drawn together with a few combs and pins. There was no colour on her face and she looked so pale that her black eyes burnt out fiercely from her white skin. Lady Penelope's lovely velvet gown of orange, Devereux pride to the last, was torn and mud-stained, and the room in which we stood was cold, dark and miserable. There was a trestle-bed against one wall and a three-legged stool in one corner. Nothing else.

'What do you need?' I asked huskily, willing myself not to cry, not to show the disgust and anger I felt for the treatment of my poor lady. 'To whom can I go for help? You cannot stay long here. It is not possible to live in these conditions, and you have done nothing wrong. They must be told to release you, at once!'

Lady Penelope managed a wry smile and put one slender hand to her head.

'Dearest Meg, it is not as easy as you may think. But I do not fear the future. I shall speak the truth and the Queen will know that I bear her complete loyalty and allegiance. What I desire most of all is someone to cook for me, for no food has been provided. Go to my husband, Meg, and beg him for some linen and wall-hangings. It is so very cold here. See Elizabeth, if you can, and find out from her what has happened to Southampton, and my brother. Dear Heavens,' she let out a sighing sob, 'how is this all to end?'

I did not stay long for there was much to do, and I could not bear the thought of my lady staying in that miserable cold, without food, for very much longer. However, Lord Rich refused to see me at his Smithfield house. Now that his brother-in-law Essex was no longer of use to him, he quickly discarded the Devereux family and joined the opposing ranks.

Evil man, I thought, as Mary and I made our weary way back to Cheap-side. For how long had he accepted his wife's immoral behaviour, without one word of restraint, or criticism? For how many years had Lord Rich accepted

Mountjoy's hold on Lady Penelope's heart, and the intrusion of bastard children into his home, allowing them to bear his name?

For eleven years, or more, he had made the most of both his wife, and his brother-in-law, because of their importance at Court. But now, the moment their prestige began to crumble, he was ready to change sides, to deny all support for his wife, and rid himself of the Devereux family almost as if they had never existed in his life.

Judas, I thought viciously, panting with rage and fatigue, and wishing that his pious, unlovely and Puritan head could be laid low at the block.

If I had possessed the courage, I would have made my way to the Palace of Whitehall and begged help for my lady there. But I was too tired and, moreover, knew neither whom to ask for assistance, nor who could be trusted at this perilous time.

So we went back to Cheapside, and I wrote many letters that night on my lady's behalf, sending messengers abroad with them to Elizabeth, Countess of Southampton, Frances, Countess of Essex, and to Dorothy, Countess of Northumberland who was, I hoped, residing at Syon House. I wanted to write to Lord Mountjoy in Ireland, but did not know how to reach him. I felt it was imperative for him to know what was happening so far away, and prayed that he would hear the news of Penelope Rich from some other source.

In answer to my pleas came one reply, but it was the one most welcome to me, and it was from Dorothy, my lady's sister.

She would inform the Privy Council, she said, of her sister's lack of food and linen, and make sure that Lord Rich was ordered to supply them. Her husband, the Earl of Northumberland, was a good friend of Raleigh's, she went on, and as Sir Walter was Captain of the Queen's Guard, he would have all the information I needed to know.

' . . . Times are bad at present,' she

wrote, 'for the Devereux family, and I am keeping myself carefully in the background for fear of what may happen. But you know where my heart lies, Meg, and I will do everything within my power to help those I love. Pray, dear Meg, pray hard for us all, and I will let you know further news as soon as I can obtain it . . . '

On the 17th February, indictments were laid by the Privy Council and a long list of names appeared of those involved in the rebellion. At the head of the list were the names of the Earl of Essex, the Earl of Southampton, and Lady Rich. Essex was charged with an attempt to usurp the Crown, and with Southampton and others, of having conspired to depose and slay the Queen and to subvert the government.

It was treason.

Essex's trial took place on the 19th February, and amongst the peers who tried him was his Judas brother-in-law, Lord Rich.

I was in a most worried and upset

state during those cold February days, for I was refused further access to Lady Penelope, awaiting examination by the Privy Council; I heard no more from Lady Dorothy, and I did not know where to turn, nor what to do. Mary was sweet and tender, bringing me morsels to eat whenever she saw me, begging me to eat and rest, but I could do neither. I travelled the streets, Essex House to the Keeper's, and on to St Bartholomews in Smithfield, then back to Essex House again. But nobody would speak to me, and I could find out nothing about my dear lady.

Then, one day, arriving back at Cheapside, totally exhausted and very cold, I found Richard Villier awaiting me. Within minutes I was undressed and bundled into bed, and a hot posset was being held to my mouth.

'I knew that you would be acting foolishly,' he said, holding my head up with one hand and forcing me to drink from the cup in his other hand. 'I knew that nobody here would be able to control you in a sensible way, and that I would be needed. You should have your bum smacked, Margaret Dawlish, and if you were not in such a weak and feeble condition I would gladly do it!'

His eyes sparked like green flames and his words were harshly spoken, but his hand was gentle as it held my head and oh, how good it was to feel loved and cared for once more.

'I need to know,' I said, turning my face away from the cup and burrowing it against his chest. 'Nobody will tell me things and I am so tired of trying, Richard. I want to know how my lady is, and what they will do to her — and — '

'That is why I am here.' He placed the cup down on the stool beside my bed and pressed me back onto my pillows, then pulled the coverlet right up to my chin. 'I will go out now and gain all the news I can, and will return with this information to Cheapside. But in so doing I must have your word,

Meg.' He rose to his feet and looked down at me, very tall, and strong, and unsmiling. 'You will give me your word now, that you will remain in bed until I return. And that you will eat and drink all that Mary brings to you.'

'I promise,' I whispered.

'And if I should be away for two days, or a week, I know not how long this will take — you will not leave this house until I return?'

'Go now, Richard Villier,' I said, 'and begin your questions.' My voice became stronger as I felt his love warming me, deep into the very core of my being. 'I promise to stay here until you come back to me, but hurry. I beg you, hurry!'

Later, I was to hear the whole sad story from Richard.

Essex and Southampton were condemned to death for treason, as was Sir Christopher Blount, the stepfather of both Essex and my Lady Penelope. Essex remained calm during his trial, but after the sentence of execution was pronounced he made a confession to Robert Cecil, betraying those about him, and particularly his sister, Lady Rich. He accused her of urging him on, of telling him that he lacked valour and that all his friends and supporters thought he was a coward. He also accused her of adultery with Lord Mountjoy. Sir Charles Danvers and his secretary, Henry Cuffe, were more that he named in the confession.

Robert Devereux, Earl of Essex, was executed on the 25th February, in the year 1601. He was executed inside the walls of the Tower of London because the Queen, it was said, feared the people's reactions to his death and would not allow a public spectacle. There had been trouble enough from the crowds when Essex had been imprisoned in York House, I remembered Richard telling me, with bawdy songs shouted in taverns all over the City, and carousing men letting out great cheers when passing York House at night. Many soldiers held fond memories of Essex, and drank confusion to his enemies, of whom hunchbacked Robert Cecil was the most hated.

So, on the day of his execution, the Queen was fearful of another uprising, and made it known that the Earl had asked for a private execution as a special favour.

Richard Villier attended at the scaffold, with but a small group of onlookers, at seven in the morning. When I asked him why he went there, he answered that as most would be there to watch an enemy die, he felt it only right to mourn as a friend.

'Not that I was ever fond of Robert Devereux,' he added swiftly, 'he caused you pain, which I can never forgive nor forget. But there were good qualities as well as bad in his tempestuous, hot-tempered nature, and it must be a terrible thing to die without a friend in sight. Raleigh was there, as Captain of the Guard, but he withdrew to the White Tower and watched from the window. I wondered a little, what he must have been thinking.'

'I hope it was quick,' I said, shuddering. 'And that he was calm at the end.'

'Essex wore a black velvet cloak over his satin doublet and hose, and begged pardon for his past sins. He removed his cloak and ruff and then repeated the Lord's Prayer before taking off his doublet. Essex was brave to the last, Meg, and refused a blindfold before lying flat upon the board and fitting his head into the notch in the block.'

'And it was quick?' I said again, feeling the tears begin to well up in my eyes. It was over now. Essex was no longer around to trouble me, or his sister, or the Queen. I swallowed hard and wiped my wet eyes.

'It took the executioner three strokes to sever the head from the body,' answered Richard quietly, 'and then it was raised high in the air to a shout of — God save the Queen.'

'Thank God,' I whispered, pressing

my face against his sleeve, 'thank God it is all over.'

Sir Christopher Blount was beheaded a few weeks later, making Lettice a widow for the third time, but Henry Cuffe, who did not possess a knighthood, was taken to Tyburn and subjected to the cruel torture of hanging, disembowelling, and quartering. The Earl of Southampton's death sentence was commuted to life imprisonment, and Lady Penelope Rich was released with no penalty whatsoever.

I could scarcely believe this, having known previously that her name was one at the head of the list of those involved in the rebellion. But Richard told me that Lady Rich had been examined by the Privy Council, and had behaved with such modesty and wisdom that the Queen had ordered her to be set at liberty.

'Your Lady Penelope must be admired for her courage,' he remarked, 'although I say that, who bear her no love. For she stood before those men who hoped to condemn her, and was entirely on her own; Mountjoy is in Ireland, Lord Rich has abandoned her, and her once adored brother betrayed her before he died. Yet she stood, so I have been informed, quietly and steadfastly, and answered all questions most calmly. She acted in the rebellion as a slave to her brother, she said, because of her exceeding love for him, and for no other reason.

'In fact, Meg, there was evidence enough to implicate her, and she is too strong a lady to act as a slave to anyone! But I believe that her connection with Mountjoy brought her freedom.'

'With Mountjoy? But he is not here — he is far away in Ireland,' I cried.

Richard nodded. 'Yet I think the Queen and her advisers must be very much aware of his strength and power. If your Penelope had been harmed, I think the consequences would have been momentous. As it is, Mountjoy is proving immensely successful, and although he begged leave to return to

England, the Queen refused permission saying that she needed him to remain in Ireland for the moment.'

'So now my poor lady is really alone,' I said slowly.

'Your poor lady is an extremely fortunate woman,' answered Richard indignantly, giving my shoulders a quick shake. 'She should have lost her head for playing such a leading role in the rebellion, and yet she walks away completely free. Do not 'poor lady' her to me, Meg Dawlish!'

'Do not scold,' I said, pulling his hands down to my breast. 'I have had enough of words which have filled my heart with repulsion and sorrow. Come and love me, Richard, that I may forget evil for a while. Tomorrow will be time enough to plan how I can help my lady in the future.'

Slowly, tenderly, he came to me — the man I loved, and who would so often be around when I most needed him. Despite his words, I knew that Lady Penelope was to be pitied and that I possessed far, far more than the beautiful Lady Rich.

For a time I heard nothing of my lady and knew only that she had gone away into the country. Then I received a letter from her, telling me that she was with her mother at Drayton Bassett.

. . . 'Dorothy is here also, and Frances,' she wrote in her small, neat writing, 'so I am not entirely alone, but miss my dearest Charles most dreadfully. We all bemoan Robert's death, but do not speak of him out aloud — the pain is still too great. Soon I shall be travelling to Wanstead, dear Meg, which Charles has recently purchased, and I would so like it if you would come there and stay with me awhile . . .'

This I did, and it was a joy to see my lady in better health and spirits, and with so many children around her. Her four by Lord Rich, however, had not been allowed to visit their mother.

'Robert is becoming more and more like his father,' she told me, with a mischievous smile, 'and a real Puritan.

So very tiring, Meg. Perhaps it is just as well that we see little of each other. But Henry is more like me, and a bright and cheerful boy. I am sorry that you cannot see him here. The girls are, of course, young ladies now, with Lettice nineteen years, and Essex, seventeen.'

Despite the absence of the Rich offspring, I saw children in plenty and took my time in getting to know the five Blounts — Penelope, Mountjoy, St John, Charles and Isabella.

'It must be sad for Lord Mountjoy to be so far away from these delights,' I said, gazing at the various childish faces. 'He must miss them all most terribly.'

'He will be home soon,' answered my lady firmly, taking little Isabella upon her lap and allowing the child's fat fingers to play with one of her dangling ear-rings. 'Next year at the latest, Charles has promised me that.'

'If the Queen will allow it,' I said. 'Lord Mountjoy is doing so well in Ireland she may not give permission for him to return.'

'The Queen is very old now and cannot last for much longer,' replied my lady quietly. 'Then, hopefully, under the new King, we can expect more understanding. Charles wants to come home now, Meg. He has this lovely home waiting for him, and everything that will give him most pleasure — his children, his library, his gardens, his pools and ponds. He loves fishing, do you remember?'

I nodded, although this was not something I had known about the gentleman.

'Charles is not really a military man,' went on Lady Penelope, 'and has used it solely as a means of advancement. He will be far happier here, reading his beloved books and walking in his beautiful gardens.'

For a man who was 'not really a military man' Lord Mountjoy proved to be a great and successful leader of men, and on Christmas Eve of the year 1601, he won a resounding victory at Kinsale.

I heard from Richard, who was jubilant at England's supremacy in Ireland, that only six English lives were lost in the battle, whilst Irish losses amounted to over one thousand.

He will come home now, I thought, and spend his days as a country gentleman with Lady Penelope and their children, at Wanstead.

But this was not to be, for we heard of a great sickness which suddenly swept over the English army and many men died, who had been untouched by the dangers of battle. Lord Mountjoy became seriously ill himself, and for a time it was believed that he would die, also. However, the great man recovered eventually and by the following Christmas it was announced that the Irish rebellion was over at long last and the rebel, Tyrone, had surrendered.

The year of 1603 was busy and eventful for my lady, and after her two years of solitude, she was more than ready to take a full part in Court life again.

Queen Elizabeth died on the 24th March, and James of Scotland took over the crown of England. Lord Mountjoy was to return home at the end of May, but before my lady saw him once more, she travelled north with other ladies of rank, to escort the new queen to London.

Lady Penelope came to see me in the shop that spring, needing more damasks and brocades, announcing that she had not nearly enough attire to wear at the newly lavish and extravagant Court.

'Queen Anne is a most pleasure-loving lady, and likes to have very young and gay females about her. I must not look my age, Meg, and will wear the most gorgeous and eye-catching apparel to please Queen Anne.'

'It will make a difference to your life after the previous dull years, my lady,' I said, showing her the rolls of popinjay green, Drake's colour and horseflesh colour, newly in from Antwerp, as well as the orange, which she adored.

'I am to be made a Lady of the Drawing Chamber, Meg, and have been invited to take a leading part in all Court occasions. Those early years of intrigue, and the letters which Robert and I wrote to the King in Scotland, have paid their reward at last!' she cried jubilantly. 'Oh, Meg, I am so happy, and will know total fulfilment when Charles returns to join me.'

When Lord Mountjoy did return, honours and grants of lands were showered upon him by the grateful King, and he was promoted to Lord Lieutenant of Ireland, and created the Earl of Devonshire, as well. My Lady Penelope lived openly with him at Wanstead, and they spent much time furnishing their home and making it a place of even greater beauty. I was happy for them both, that at last they could find tranquillity and contentment in their life together, but, as always, with my vivacious and fun-loving lady, such happiness was not to last for long.

Was she too like a star, I wondered,

wishing that life would treat her more kindly. Was she, indeed, to be Sir Philip Sidney's 'Stella' all her days? Sometimes rising, and sometimes falling to earth like a meteorite?

14

It was Lady Dorothy who warned me of approaching danger this time, not Richard Villier, and she begged me to see her sister and try to talk some sense into her.

'She loves you, Meg, and will, I think, listen to you more readily than to any other being, apart from Charles.'

'Dearie me, what is it now?' I asked, looking at the Countess of Northumberland's worried face, and thinking that this Devereux daughter, though younger than her sister, was showing her age rather more than the beautiful Lady Rich.

The Countess was wearing saffron yellow taffeta over a cartwheel hoop, and her double peplum stuck straight out below her waist, making a somewhat large impression of her figure. Lady Dorothy looked old and tired and unhappy, and I wondered if her marriage was causing her trouble, as Lady Penelope had once feared it would.

'I saw Lady Penelope but a few weeks ago,' I went on, 'and she was busily purchasing material here. She was so excited about being at Court again, and said that the new queen was showing her every kindness and favour.'

'That is part of the trouble,' answered Lady Dorothy, 'for Penelope is spending too much time at Court and not enough with Charles.'

'But is he not with her? I assumed that he spent just as much time there as my lady. The King is said to be delighted with Lord Mountjoy and has showered him with just rewards.'

'The King!' Lady Dorothy almost spat out the word. 'King James is a revolting man and I wish that you could see him, Meg, then you would believe me. He is afraid of water so never washes his body, his personal smell is quite dreadful, and he is never without his favourites.'

'But Queen Elizabeth always had her favourites — as we were well aware, madam,' I said. 'It must surely be a Royal whim.'

Lady Dorothy looked at me with an expression of disgust.

'These favourites are all male, whom he touches and caresses in public, all the time. How they do not faint from the appalling stench, I do not know, save that they are surrounded by every conceivable pouncet-box and pomander.'

'Oh,' I said. Lady Penelope had said nothing of this, and she was a most clean and fastidious lady. But then she had not spoken much about the King at all; her main topic of conversation was of Queen Anne, and of the clothing worn and most admired at Court.

'Of course,' went on the Countess, 'much must be accepted, much forgotten, because he is King. And Penelope is managing to both accept and forget very nicely. But it is Mountjoy whom I worry about, Meg. He is a great soldier, and has withstood so much in the way of violence and bloodshed and slaughter. He is disciplined and gentle, well-mannered and brave, intelligent and dignified. Yet our new Earl of Devonshire stays away from Court as much as he decently can, because he hates the mounting scandal and corruption there.'

'Lady Penelope certainly gave me no idea of all this, madam. To her, the Court was magnificent once more after her years away from it. Why cannot Lord Mountjoy speak to her, and get her to realise that it is not the right place for her, or for him?'

Lady Dorothy shrugged. 'Maybe he does not want to spoil her pleasure, for Penelope is enjoying herself, no doubt of that. Or perhaps he thinks that she will gradually become bored with all the lavish splendour. But I worry about Charles, for since his long illness in Ireland he does not look as fit as he should, and I feel Penelope should spend more time with him, and their children, at Wanstead.'

'And you believe *I* am the right person to tell Lady Penelope that? Why can you not advise your own sister, madam?'

I did not speak harshly, nor did I mean any impertinence to the Countess, and fortunately she accepted my words in good heart.

'Oh, Meg, you have been with us Devereuxs for so long that you are even thought of as family! I dare not speak to Penelope because, as usual, my dear husband is causing trouble. You know that he and Sir Walter Raleigh have always been friends? Well, Raleigh is now in the Tower again and likely to remain there, and Northumberland is disliked by King James, though trying hard and unsuccessfully to win His Majesty's affection.

'If I should dare to criticise Penelope, she would doubtless imagine that I was speaking from envy, wishing that I, too, could lead the exciting life at Court which she enjoys.'

'I will do my best,' I answered, 'but it is unlikely that my lady will listen to me.'

In fact, I did not get the chance to speak to Lady Penelope on the matter, for she became so involved with the Court at that time that I did not see her again for many months.

Richard Villier, like the Earl of Devonshire, spent as little time at Court as possible, but from him I heard of my lady's triumphs in performing the many masques so adored by the new queen.

In the January of 1604, 'The Vision of the Twelve Goddesses' was performed in the Great Hall at Hampton Court, and the Queen, herself, appeared as the Goddess of Wisdom. Lady Penelope took the role of Venus, Goddess of Love, and wore a loose, flowing garment of embroidered satin, and cloth of gold and silver. She looked extremely beautiful, Richard told me, and very much younger than her forty-one years.

The Queen, he said, surprised imagination by wearing a garment so short that it scarcely covered her knees. Afterwards, the entertainers invited members of the audience to join them in the dance, and he saw Lord Mountjoy treading the more sedate measures, with little pleasure showing on his gaunt face.

The following year I hoped that my lady would change her lifestyle and settle down permanently at Wanstead, for I received a brief, excited letter from her, telling me that Lord Rich had at long last commenced divorce proceedings against her.

. . . 'a lawful marriage is what Charles and I most desire,' she wrote, 'and he will not be completely satisfied until he is able to pass on his earldom to young Mountjoy, and his great fortune to all his children, in a right and legal manner. I am agreeing with Lord Rich on every matter, Meg, so that he may obtain his divorce quickly, and thus free me. But I will not allow the name of

Devonshire to be dragged through the courts, so have confessed to adultery with a stranger . . . '

Judgement was given on the 14th November, 1605, and the judges pronounced sentence of divorce, warning that the couple must not remarry, but must live chastely and celibately in the future.

I could not believe that such a ruling was possible, and wrote hastily to Lady Dorothy, asking her if it was indeed right that Lady Penelope, as a divorced lady, was not legally allowed to remarry.

It was foolish of me to have pestered the Countess of Northumberland with questions at that time, for she, poor lady, was heavily involved herself with worries over her husband. The Earl of Northumberland had been implicated in the Gunpowder Plot, on the 5th November, condemned to pay the huge sum of thirty-thousand pounds, and to life imprisonment in the Tower. No doubt she was busily engaged in writing letters, as she had had to do in the past as Thomas Perrot's wife, begging for her husband's release.

Understandably, I received no reply from Lady Dorothy, and it was not until the New Year that I heard the unwelcome news. Lady Penelope Rich and the Earl of Devonshire had been married on the 26th December, at Wanstead.

Later, my lady was to explain to me that under the old Queen's reign, divorced couples were allowed to remarry. Both she and the Earl had known of the stricter rules under King James, but had believed that their marriage would be allowed if they paid a large sum of money in penalty.

Charles, she told me, had written long and learned letters to the King, in defence of his marriage, but the King was not impressed. He had particularly turned against Lady Penelope, telling her husband that he had won a fair woman with a black soul. She was no longer to appear at Court, although the Earl was to continue with his official duties. But in King James' eyes, the Earl of Devonshire had been dishonoured by his illegal marriage.

Richard was very angry when he heard the news; although he had never cared for Penelope Rich, he had great admiration for Lord Mountjoy and none whatsoever for King James.

'The King has made strict laws relating to divorce because of the appalling decadence at Court,' he said. 'His Majesty wishes to appear highly defensive of moral standards in public — so that his people should never know about his own sexual behaviour. I feel great sympathy for Mountjoy, Meg. He is such a good man, I pray that this illegal marriage will not break his heart.'

In the spring of the following year, Richard's ominous words were proved correct. One day in March, the Earl and Countess of Devonshire, as I was trying to remember to call them, were in London and came to me in Cheapside to purchase several sticks of arras for their home in Wanstead. My lady was particularly interested in the ones depicting Biblical stories, which I had recently received from Antwerp, and the Earl agreed with her choice. They left me with a comfortable sum of money in my purse, and requests to go and stay with them at Wanstead when I could spare the time.

As they were leaving and climbing into the great coach which would bear them homewards, now beautifully emblazoned with the new Devonshire arms, I remembered Lady Dorothy's words to me and thought that Mountjoy did not look well.

The Earl of Devonshire was more stooped, and did not hold his tall figure in the old, erect manner; his face had lost both width and colour, to my watchful eyes, and appeared shrunken and more like a man ten years older than he was.

Lady Penelope, Countess of Devonshire, looked as radiant as ever and I felt no fears for her. Despite not being allowed at Court any longer, she looked happy, and very much in love with the man who was at last her husband.

Now, I thought, waving them on their way, now my lady has no excuse to leave her home and will find contentment in the country with her family around her.

Two days later, on the 25th March, I was surprised to see the Devonshire coach passing through Cheapside once more, and to hear a few hours later from Rowland, that the Earl had been taken ill and was resting at Savoy House, in the Strand.

'I have heard that things are bad for him, mistress,' said Rowland, 'for he has sent for his lawyer and his doctor, and there is a great hurry and scurry going on there.'

'Is the Countess with him?' I asked, knowing that Lady Dorothy had been right in believing him to be unwell, but praying that Mountjoy's health would recover, as it had done in Ireland.

Rowland went to ascertain further

and came back with the news that the Earl had travelled on his own to London, with only his secretary in attendance, and on leaving home he had been in good health.

The following day Lady Penelope came up to join her husband at Savoy House, and their eldest son, Mountjoy, accompanied her. Once I knew that my lady was there, I went at once to Savoy House and asked if the Countess of Devonshire would see me. She wanted me there, as I thought she would, and I was to remain with my lady for almost two weeks.

It was clear to me, and to all those present, that the Earl had little time left of life. He must also have realised this himself, for he called for his lawyers, eight witnesses to his will, and many trusted friends, and whilst his doctor prescribed the taking of physic and much letting of blood, the Earl of Devonshire spent those last days putting his affairs in order.

Lady Penelope and I remained in

the top gallery, with young Mountjoy, and watched for seemingly endless hours as the Earl read and signed document after document in the hall beneath us.

On the final day I saw my lady give her dearly beloved husband a last embrace, kissing his hands and face before he died in her arms. The Earl remained calm to the very end, and called her his 'angel' with his last breath.

The Earl of Devonshire died of a burning fever and putrefaction of his lungs, on the 3rd April, at the age of forty-three.

I stayed with my lady for several more days, for she lay, dressed in mourning with her golden hair shrouded in a veil, in one corner of the bedchamber, and would neither move nor speak, eat or drink. She did not weep but lay as if dead herself, in a state of abject misery.

Her mother was there, and her sister, Dorothy, as well as her sister-in-law,

Frances, and we all spoke to her and comforted her, begging her to arise and continue with her life, for the children needed her. Young Mountjoy was particularly entreating in his own sadness, and he, it was, who finally pulled Lady Penelope to her feet. Slowly she gathered her wits and her courage, and we were able to make her take some sustenance.

My dear lady, who had found perfect happiness for such a very short time in her tempestuous life. And, once the Earl of Devonshire was dead, she had yet more unpleasantness to contend with, for her husband had died an extremely wealthy man, and several distant relatives came forward to stake their claims on the inheritance. Some months later, when I went to stay with her at Wanstead, Lady Penelope told me of all the difficulties which had arisen during the very start of her widowhood.

'There are a series of legal battles going on now, Meg, disputing my marriage with Charles, and the legitimacy of our children. And, even worse, is the fact that the validity of his will is being questioned, as well as all the documents which he signed and put in order that last week of his life.'

'But what are they saying?' I cried. 'The Earl had witnesses in plenty for I saw them at Savoy House, and all his lawyers were there, too.'

Lady Penelope sighed. 'It is being said that Charles was of unsound mind when he made his will; then it is being claimed that *I* forced him to make the will in my favour, and that I am not legally his widow; other voices shout that the will and documents have been tampered with. Oh, Meg — I thought that after the indignity of his funeral I would have to face no more accusations, or insults. But it seems as if trouble shadows me relentlessly. Sometimes I wish that I could have taken my dear husband's hand and travelled with him on the third of April, to a much happier and gentler land.'

I leaned forward and took both her cold hands in mine; so white and dead they looked, lying like marble upon the black satin of her gown.

'Do not speak so, my lady. You have always had courage and will find it again now, to strengthen and uphold you. What befell at the funeral? Tell me about it.'

'Charles was honoured with a state funeral at Westminster Abbey, in recognition of his great services to his country. But during the preparations the Court heralds decided not to acknowledge me as the Countess of Devonshire.' Lady Penelope stopped speaking and swallowed hard. Then her fingers entwined themselves in mine. 'At the funeral ceremony I was humiliated in public, for the Earl's coat of arms were set up 'in single' without mine. He possessed no wife, you see.'

'That makes me very angry but it is all over and done with now, and best forgotten. *You* know that he loved you, and that you were his wife, so do all his friends. I take it that both you, and the children, have been well cared for in your husband's will, and have no financial problems?'

Lady Penelope nodded. 'I have been given an interest for life in all Charles' lands and estates, and after my death they are to go to the children, and then to their heirs. Oh, it is all most generous and perfect, Meg, *if* the will is declared valid.'

'It will be,' I answered firmly, 'it must be.'

On the 22nd November, I heard that the will was upheld by the Prerogative Court of Canterbury, and although there was an appeal against this decision in the Consistory Court at St Paul's Cathedral in May of the following year, once again the will was declared valid.

'That will be that then,' I said to Richard Villier, who had come up to see me, and attend to some business in London that spring. 'I really believe now that the whole miserable matter will be forgotten, and Lady Penelope and her children can start life afresh and in confidence about their future.'

'I fear not, my darling Meg,' replied Richard, looking most soberly at me, 'for criminal charges have now been brought against your Penelope, and three of the lawyers involved in the making of Devonshire's will. And they are being accused in the Court of Star Chamber, which is known for its dislike of women, and for interrogations which are loaded with questions based on false premises.'

I felt my heart lurch downwards as if it would leave my body, and clutched both hands to my breast to try and control it.

'What do you know about the proceedings there?' I whispered.

'I know only that accusations of forging the will and documents have been brought against Lady Penelope and the lawyers. These accusations, if proved correct, carry penalties of imprisonment for life, forfeiture of all lands and goods, and slitting of nostrils,' he replied. 'Ten years ago, your Penelope's brother, the Earl of Essex, was one of the judges on a similar case of forgery, and the accused received life imprisonment, as well as having both his ears cut off.'

'Dear Heavens!' I cried out. 'Will this torture never end for her? Was losing her husband not enough for my lady, and must she be physically punished as well? And for *what*, Richard? What has my lady ever done to deserve such ill-treatment?'

'She did not play by the rules, Meg, you must understand that. She committed adultery, and with a very famous man, so that her deed can never be forgotten or, indeed, forgiven.'

'But Mountjoy was at fault, too!'

'The Earl of Devonshire was not married,' said Richard quietly, 'and, what is more, Devonshire is now dead.'

'So his poor, lonely widow must be made to bear the consequences?'

'He was also an extremely wealthy

man, and riches are always envied, and grabbed by every possible means.'

'Hence such vile court proceedings,' I said bitterly.

'Yes, indeed,' answered Richard, coming to me and taking me into his strong arms. 'You will need every ounce of strength, and all your calm good sense, in the following weeks, Meg. For proceedings have begun in the Star Chamber, and Lady Penelope will have to fight for her life, I fear.'

* * *

It is difficult for me to write further on this evil matter, save to say that my lady held herself with dignity and self-possession, denying all charges and insisting that she had been most maliciously slandered. She had been named in the action as Penelope, Lady Rich, but she would not accept this as her rightful name. She was not allowed to use the title, Countess of Devonshire, so she became simply Lady

Penelope, as I had always known her, and possessed no surname.

Court cases such as these could drag on for a considerable length of time, but once my lady had given her calm and firm reply on the 19th May, she had no further part in the proceedings and was able to retire to the country.

A few weeks later, in the midsummer of that fateful year, she became ill of a fever. On the 7th July, in the year 1607, Lady Penelope died, in her forty-fourth year.

It was never clear to me what caused my lady's death, for she had had colds and fevers in the past from which she had recovered, and she had even been laid low by the dread smallpox, and yet had survived. But, I always feel, Lady Penelope was low in spirit that year, having been branded a harlot and a dangerous schemer, intent on getting her hands upon the Devonshire fortune, and I believe that her wonderful courage failed her at the last, and she died from a broken heart with no man to love and protect her.

I was not told of either her sickness, or her death in Westminster, until some weeks later, and for that I can never forgive her mother, or her sister, or her sister-in-law, all of whom knew of my love for Lady Penelope, and hers for me.

I did attend her burial, however, and Richard came with me.

It took place at All Hallows, Barking by the Tower, on the 7th October, and her tombstone bore the saddest inscription of all, 'Here Lies a Lady Devereux'.

For some days I could not stop myself from weeping, and it was only my dear Richard who kept me sane, in my feelings of extreme anger and despair.

He explained that Lord Rich had long since disowned my lady, so there would have been no place for her in the Rich family tomb in Essex. Nor could she have been buried with her second husband, the Earl of Devonshire, for his body was at Westminster Abbey, with his coat of arms 'in single'. So, the only place for my dear lady was in a Devereux burial-ground and there, at All Hallows, she joined her grandfather.

'But no proper name,' I sobbed, still remembering the words of a scandalous epitaph which I had seen on one of the broadsheets printed soon after her death:

'Here lieth Penelope or my Lady
    Rich
Or my Lady of Devonshire, I
    know not which.
She shuffled, she cut, she dealt,
    she played,
She died neither wife, widow nor
    maid.
One stone contains her: this death
    can do,
Which in her life, was not content
    with two.'

'Both her Rich sons were old enough to have a say in the funeral arrangements,' said Richard gently, holding me very close, 'and they doubtless found their mother an embarrassment to them. Robert, as you know, is a strong Puritan, and everything Lady Penelope did is against his beliefs. And Henry, so I have been told, intends becoming a great courtier — perhaps a more fortunate one than his Uncle Robert? But with no desire for an end such as the Earl of Essex experienced, he would not have wanted to remind King James of his disgraced mother.'

'I hate them — hate them all!' I cried, digging my fingers into Richard's broad shoulders and wishing that I could get my hands around their self-righteous necks — *all* their necks.

'Hush now and calm yourself,' said Richard firmly, removing my clinging fingers from his doublet and brushing them with his lips. 'You loved her and can remember her always with affection. That is all that matters now, Meg. Your Lady Penelope has joined her Charles, and they will be happy together, and nobody can ever hurt them again.'

'No,' I said, and sniffed. 'Nobody can hurt her, or slander her again.' And the thought comforted me.

'Now,' said Richard's voice above my head, 'may I speak to you about Margaret Dawlish for a change?'

I smiled and rubbed my wet face against his doublet. 'Yes, dear Richard, and I will try and pay attention to you. You have been so very patient with me in the past, and I promise now to concentrate on you. There is, after all, nobody else to care for now.'

He pushed me away from him and looked down at me with a most strange expression in his eyes. 'Then at last I may say something I have been wanting to say for some time. Meg Dawlish, will you marry me?'

My mouth fell open and I felt as if my eyes would burst out of my head.

'Do not mock me, Richard Villier. You have a wife already! Or are you hoping to behave like my Lady

Penelope and divorce one before taking on another? *Shame* on you for talking such rubbish!'

'Meg,' he caught hold of my hands again and gave me a shake, 'Meg, listen to me. My wife is dead — she died over a year ago in childbirth, but you were so engrossed with your Penelope I could not tell you.'

'Maud is dead?' I was dumbfounded.

'Yes, my little Maud died in 1605 and it was a sad day for me, although I never loved her as I should.'

'But why didn't you *tell* me?' I still could not believe his words.

'Because you never asked about her, or my children, or my home in Shropshire. Because you were too busy with your own affairs here in London. Because I have lived two lives for a long time now, and always tried to keep them quite separate. Because I wanted you, Meg, have always wanted you, but could not speak sensibly to you until you were in the right frame of mind.'

'How strange,' I said softly, 'that the

two people we loved have gone from us, leaving us both alone. Perhaps it is God's will?'

'Then will you marry me, Meg?'

'Yes,' I said.

There was nothing now that I would like more. I was sick of London; sick of the callous people, the cruelty, the striving for favours and ambition; sick of the stench from the open sewers in the streets, sick of the noise outside my windows, and the plague which was an annual visitor to the city.

'I am ready now to live in the country, and lead a quiet, ordinary life,' I said slowly. 'And I am honoured that you should want me, Richard Villier.'

'I want you for my children,' he replied, smiling. 'I have five now, although you have never asked about them, and they badly need a mother.'

'And you?' I said, putting my hands up to his bearded face and looking into his bright green eyes. 'Do you want me for your own sake, Richard? Or as an organiser of your household, and a carer of your children?'

'I want you, too, Meg Dawlish, and you should know that by now. I want you in my bed, and in my arms, always.'

On St Stephen's Day, in the year 1607, I married Richard Villier in the village of Longville, in Shropshire. It was the same date as my lady had been married, although two years later, and I was fortunate in receiving nothing but happiness and joy in my married life.

Sadly, I never bore Richard a child, but there were sons and daughters enough to take up my time and my affections in our Shropshire home. And in some strange way, the fact that I was barren seemed to draw my husband and me even closer together. Maud's children were always there to cherish, and to reprimand, if necessary, but Richard and I were complete in ourselves, and in our great love for one another.

I sold my shop in Cheapside for a fine sum of money, so was able to go to Richard with a dowry of which to be proud. The merchant was willing to take on Rowland, and the other lads, for which I was thankful. But Nellie Frost and Mary Tredworthy both decided to face the depths of the Shropshire countryside with me, and they remain with me to this day.

So I end this tale, not so much the history of Margaret Villier, born Dawlish, but that of Lady Penelope, born Devereux. Life did not treat her kindly, but she knew true love during her trouble-filled days, and for that I shall always be glad.

Grateful, too, that I was part of her life and a witness to both the rising and the falling of Sir Philip Sidney's 'Stella'.

THE END

RHAPSODY OF LOVE

Rachel Ford

When painter Maggie Sanderson found herself trapped in the same Caribbean hideaway as world-famous composer Steve Donellan, she was at a loss what to do. She tried to distance herself from him, but he seemed determined to make his presence felt, crashing his way around the house day and night. Was there no way she could find peace from this man, or was he going to ruin her sanity too, as he had ruined everything else?